MY HUSBAND THE MURDERER

CHARLOTTE BARNES

BLOODHOUND BOOKS

Print ISBN: 978-1-917449-24-3

Mum –
In every good mother I write, there's you.

ONE

It had always made me feel better to have a list.

I had fond memories of the food shop with my mother when I was young. The ways in which we would wander the aisles together, and she would haphazardly put things into the basket without planning or forethought. But when we arrived at the checkout and inevitably found that there wasn't enough money in my mother's purse to pay for the jumbo packet of kitchen roll *and* the apples, satsumas and raisins that would go into my lunchbox, I would always side-eye the women in the checkouts next to us – clutching their lists. They would ease through the checkout process, bagging their purchases with speed and efficiency. Meanwhile, my mother would be staring down at her unbagged, unbought items, wondering whether she could possibly choose between the fresh fish that might form part of my father's dinner that evening, and the white, branded bread – rather than supermarket brand – that would form my week's worth of sandwiches for school.

'They're so funny, aren't they? It can be impossible to know what to get.'

A stranger's voice wrangled me free from the memory of my

mother, arguing with a cashier over yogurt-covered banana pieces, and back into the present day. Here, I was holding a value packet of boxed raisins that I did not, would not need, in one hand, while clutching my list – where my raisins weren't – with the other hand. I put them back on the shelf and laughed.

'Sometimes things grab your attention when you don't even need them.'

The woman waved a hand as though to brush away the comment, but then she agreed with it all the same. 'I'm terrible for it. But for what it's worth,' she reached forwards and grabbed a six-pack of raisins and nut mix, 'my two are especially fond of these.' I took the packet from her, though I had no intention of buying them. I wondered whether she thought I was buying for children. *No, no*, I realised, *too old for that*. Grandchildren, maybe. 'Actually, while I'm here,' she grabbed a second packet and threw them into her heaving trolley, 'may as well.' She smiled and shrugged and walked on down the aisle.

That, I thought, is a woman without a list.

Otis and Finn hadn't been fussy eaters when they were children, which had made food shopping for them much easier. Now, as adults, I felt I didn't know them well enough to gauge their tastes for things. I had onions, garlic, carrots, swede, lentils. It would make a wholesome cottage pie for when they visited later in the week, and I thought they could both take portions home for their partners, too. Partners, not wives, even though Otis had been coupled for some ten years now and Finn had been with his beau for nearly six. I always invited Emilia and Alice but they seldom came; the boys said it was nice to spend time together as a family. Though I couldn't grasp why they weren't including their partners in our family unit; why they had always insisted on such a clean break.

'I've forgotten spinach,' I said quietly to myself as I scanned down to the bottom of the list. I would need to go back to the beginning of the shop for that, or collect it on my way to the checkout which, in terms of time – I checked my watch – would make more sense. I was shopping on a lunch break and although there was no one at home, waiting for my green symbols on Microsoft Teams or some other godforsaken system, I still preferred to keep to my times.

I moved through the last of the chilled section and ticked things from the list as I went – full-fat milk for the recipe, skimmed for tea, butter, mature cheese – and then circled back to collect a bag of fresh spinach which I dropped onto the loaf of bread in the child's fold-out seat of my trolley. It was another methodological decision, to keep things separated out as I might like to pack them. Hard and chilled at one end of the shopping trolley; soft and prone to damage, or at the very least being squashed, at the other. My mother never did that either, only waited for the bread to regain its buoyancy or for the crumpets to spring back into shape when she'd unpacked them at home.

The checkout line was uncharacteristically long for this time of day. I didn't go through the self-service, where people on their official lunch breaks were buying Meal Deals that they likely couldn't afford the luxury of these days but bought them all the same for the convenience of it. I went through a real checkout with a real person who might ask about my day and what my plans were for the rest of it. I never forced the conversation, but I was always glad when it came. Though you can have too much of a good thing – here, the easy conversation with a stranger being the good thing – as I came to realise when it occurred to me that I was queueing behind the woman with the raisins and nuts; the woman without a list. She was piling things onto the conveyor belt ahead of me and when she was finished she turned to place down a separator, to mark the end of her shopping and the beginning of mine. I nodded and thanked her.

'You didn't go for the raisins then?'

I looked up and caught her eyeing my decisions. 'No, not in the end.'

'Probably for the best. Mine like them but they'll probably have changed their minds about them by the time I've got things home and unpacked.' She laughed but the noise sounded sad and defeated. It was the noise that tired mothers made; I remembered it. 'Your kids look a lot healthier than mine from this,' she tapped the lentils. 'Mine will only eat healthy things if they're disguised as something else. Can you deep-fry lentils?'

I knew she was joking, but I resented the categorisation of foods into healthy and unhealthy; good and bad. Lentils would probably be bad for you if you lived on them exclusively. Meanwhile, cake was only bad for you if you ate it as a main meal every day. I had tried to teach the boys that, too, though I was never sure how much of it they'd carried into adulthood. Emilia and Alice were slight things and I could imagine that both of them might pick off the melted cheese from the top of any cottage pie portions that I sent home for them. I could make them individual portions, of course, without the cheese on at all. But I worried they would take that as a criticism, as though I were depriving them or deciding for them what they should and should not have. I shook the worry away and carried on with my unloading, finishing with the small brown loaf and the spinach.

'It's terrible that business, isn't it?'

I checked my watch again before I looked up. I only had eighteen minutes to get through, get packed and get home. The woman wasn't looking at my shopping anymore, but to somewhere behind me and off to the left. When I followed her gaze I saw that she was staring at the newspapers on a nearby stand; their headlines all variations of the same thing.

'O'CONNOR READY FOR DEATHBED'
'DEATHBED CONFESSION CLAIMS MADE BY
KILLER'
'O'CONNOR: A LIFE SENTENCE AT LAST'

'I tell you something, they should have given him the death penalty when they tried him. I know we don't do it, or haven't for a long time, but God. I've got two girls and the thought of that man getting a hold of either of them.' She made a noise and I imagined her shuddering; I was still fixed on the newspapers. 'You can't think on it for too long without your heart breaking for the mothers, can you?'

Over the years I had become too familiar with different kinds of heartbreak. I wondered whether it was worse, somehow, if you were the mother to two daughters than to two sons. I wasn't close enough to read the small print underneath the headlines. Up until now I had managed to avoid taking note of them altogether. It had been years, but I could remember Edward O'Connor being caught; the reveal of that first murder and the sordid string of them that stretched out after it. I looked to the woman in front of me then and I tried to guess how many years separated us. There was a chance that she would have been only a teenager when he broke headlines the first time around; too young, perhaps, to appreciate the magnitude of the man's crimes. But I wondered whether she had heard her parents speaking of them in hushed tones in the kitchen late at night, or huddled in front of the television, their arms wrapped tightly around each other while they talked of the ways they needed to protect their child.

'Hello, can I help?' the cashier said, calling the woman along, and I was glad of it.

'Sorry, in my own world.' She hurried through with her Bags for Life, unfolding one after the other as she loaded away

Quavers and ready meals and tins of tuna and salmon. There was no rhyme or reason to how she packed. When I saw her file away a loaf of bread and place peppers, mushrooms, and a cucumber on top, I felt a small and strangled sound rise in the back of my throat that I tried desperately to swallow. There were certain things that, once deformed, could never take back their original shape.

TWO

The cottage pies needed another fifteen minutes in the oven, I thought, judging by the slow bubbles that were erupting from their corners. It was always an extra fifteen minutes for these ones, sizeable enough to feed a family. Each small pop of gravy reminded me of the mashed potato volcanoes I made for Otis and Finn when they were younger. I would spend more time than absolutely necessary moulding the potatoes into a mound before puncturing a hole in the top to excavate as much of the filling as I could. Then, just before serving, I would pour a mixture of peas, carrots and gravy that was too thick – such was their preference – to create an outpouring from the spout of the potato, allowing the lava mixture to tumble out onto their turkey dinosaurs, chicken nuggets, beef rounds.

I closed the oven door and went back to ferreting through the cupboards for more Tupperware containers. It was a mild addiction that I fed too often whenever I stared into the abyss of a shopping channel for longer than advised. Before I knew what was happening I would find myself reading out the long card number, or typing it into my phone's keypad, and then four to seven days later – depending on the urgency I felt for something new – a box of plastic would arrive on my doorstep and I would have to find a home in the kitchen for its contents. Yet somehow, whenever it came to finding the containers again I would never be able to place them until three slammed doors into searching.

There was a family of different sized ones lurking at the back of what used to be the soup cupboard. Behind them – 'Aha!' – another family that were all the same dimensions. I struggled and shoved to get them out and then lined them up across the countertop. All ten of them sat an equal distance from each other.

My list was on the kitchen table still, and I went to add a tick alongside "Find containers". All that was left now was to wait for the remainder of the cooking time. It had taken me five minutes to find the boxes, so in the remaining ten I decided to flick on the radio, fill the kettle, and stare longingly into the garden that was still frosted over, despite it being mid-morning. I pulled a teabag free of the caddy and added it to the cup once the water had boiled, and then went back to my gazing. The garden was smaller than the one at the house where I'd raised the boys, which I was thankful for. If it had been the same size then I never would have managed the upkeep alone.

'We're talking crime and punishment today...' The radio was background noise while I cradled my mug and mentally listed the plants that would need to be tended to once the frost had eased. Any day now, they said on the weather channel, though they were often wrong. 'That's right, crime and punishment, and we'll be opening the phone lines later on for you to call in with your thoughts on the matters discussed too.'

'But of course, if we're talking crime that must mean we're going to be talking about–'

I slammed my palm on the off button with such a force that the radio wavered on the window ledge. 'Everything is so bloody dark these days,' I mumbled. Whenever I spoke like this I thought of my mother doing the same; speaking quietly to herself while she cooked or sorted through piles of washing. She had done the same during her late stages of dementia. It was a strange thing to miss.

When the steam of my tea started to diminish I took three hearty mouthfuls before setting it down and going back to the oven. Both pies had cooked to a golden brown so I left the oven door partly open for the heat to drift out. It would warm the kitchen, too, which was where I spent so much of my time these days. The table had been overtaken by notebooks and workbooks and sticky notes. My bread and butter was content writing work but I was assisting with a developmental edit on a novel at the moment – though it was work that had landed on me, rather than being sought out. In the mess of the tabletop there was only one space clear; a place setting I saved for my meals.

I took my time in finishing my tea, to allow the pies time to cool, too, and then I spent the rest of the morning packaging them into containers and loading those containers into two hemp bags that would bear their weight.

One after the other the boys had cancelled, their phone calls seven minutes apart.

I didn't always go to this much effort when I was going down to the shelter. Though my weekly trips to the shelter didn't often coincide with my sons cancelling dinner plans after my having bought the ingredients to feed them. The greyscale lining in that particular cloud was that the food wouldn't go to waste at least. When I arrived the centre was already heaving, and it occurred to me that my twenty portions of cottage pie likely wouldn't even knock the smallest of dents in the cold bodies here that needed warming with a hot meal. There were crowds already clustered around the food stations, where workers were brandishing gloves and hairnets and wide smiles that could in no way counteract the daily horrors that had forced these many people to seek solace and sustenance in this hollow building. Still, a smile could often turn someone's day; it wouldn't make a one-hundred-and-eighty degree difference, but it could perhaps make things appear slightly more upright.

'Can I pop these under a heat lamp?' I asked one of the other volunteers. She ushered me behind the counter and pointed to a food station that was only half-full of meals still. She was too busy serving up what looked like portions of lasagne to make pleasantries with me and I found that I didn't mind, which must have meant that my mood was worse than I'd first realised. I didn't go to the effort of talking to anyone else; only clipped free the lids of each container and one by one slid them onto the station, under the glowing warmth of the lights overhead. There was a box of gloves and hairnets behind me that I helped myself to, before I was backed into the corner of seeking out a superior to ask where I could start.

Everything here was home-made – by someone. There were local restaurants that donated whole trays of hot meals to be distributed, along with local individuals, like myself, who cooked by the batch. It inevitably meant that there was no one single smell that could be enjoyed, but many and all at once; between that and the chatter of the many people in attendance, the room was an assault on the senses. It meant that I didn't even hear Claire when she called my name from behind, and it was only when she set a hand on my shoulder that my muscles tensed and I turned.

'Oh,' I smiled then, a real and genuine one, 'I needed a chief operator,' I joked.

'I didn't think we'd see you this week,' she said in a

questioning tone, but I only shrugged. 'But as always,' she gestured to the room around us, 'I'm always grateful for an extra pair of hands around here.' Claire was the convener for food shelters around the city; she was also notoriously cheerful. I had often wondered whether she went home, turned her phone off, and refused to smile at anyone in her personal life, as though storing energy reserves for the next day or evening at work. Though I may have been judging her by my own standards. 'Oh wow, is this what you brought?'

Claire had circled me back to where I started and I nodded. 'Lentil cottage pie.'

'Please,' came a voice from across the counter to us. There was a man wearing too many clothes, none of which looked fit to keep him warm. He held out his tray and flashed a smile that was punctuated by missing incisors.

'I'll leave you to make a start?' She squeezed my shoulder and I tensed again, but I managed to smile with it. 'Nora brought the fish pie that's alongside your meals, so feel free to dish that out, too, and just give me a shout if need be.'

I was already transferring a portion of cottage pie from glass container to paper plate. The man in front held his tray out for me to place the food onto. In the time it took me to turn around, ferret free a spork from a nearby box of them, and turn back, he had started to dig into the food with his bare hands. He paused to blow the heat from his fingers before hungrily starting again with another mouthful.

'This is bloody beautiful.'

The smile I gave him was much more authentic. There was something comforting in seeing the food enjoyed; in seeing an effort that hadn't, after all, gone to waste. 'Please, take this and find yourself a warm seat somewhere.' I handed over the plastic cutlery. 'You'll get indigestion if you eat standing up.'

He took the spork with gravy-stained hands, nodded in

thanks and then moved on. Seconds later he was replaced by another visitor, and another. The cottage pie was soon on its final portions, and I found I was steering people towards the fish pie instead. Their idle chatter and polite conversation was enough to keep my mind occupied for short bursts. But an hour into the serving another conversation became magnified. There were two volunteers talking somewhere nearby; I didn't turn to seek them out, only carried on with my assigned duties. Their comments came in waves, though, small but loud things lapping at the edge of my hearing – 'I think it's disgraceful they're giving him the time of day.' – and try as I might, I couldn't unhear – '... the poor parents all these years later.'

'Fish pie, please.'

'He'll take it to his grave otherwise.'

'I'll have fish pie an' all. Please and ta.'

'They should hear him out and then put him down. Bloody animal.'

'Is there any cottage pie left?'

'All those girls...'

'Excuse me? I asked about the cottage pie.'

THREE

There had been a lot of address changes over the years. It was never too far, but far enough to lose touch with people. Rebecca was the closest thing I had to a long-term friend. She lived a fifty-minute drive away and she had, despite my efforts against it, stuck with me through two house moves. When I moved in here three years ago, I soon gave up trying to cut any ties with her and I admitted that yes, perhaps it would be nice to know someone who had seen my last two living rooms.

The living room was where we usually lingered for our evenings together, owing to my kitchen table – that being the closest thing I had to a dining table – being covered with work materials. Rebecca didn't mind though – or if she did, she hid it well. She made herself comfortable with a bowl of home-made egg fried rice in one hand and a glass of red in the other. Rebecca pulled her legs up underneath her on the sofa, set the wine on a nearby side table and started to eat.

'I forgot, I bought prawn crackers.' I'd made an additional trip to the supermarket that lunchtime, specifically to get them. It had also been a good excuse to leave the house, to stare at the headlines. I hadn't turned the radio on in four days.

I set a bowl of crackers on the sofa cushion next to Rebecca and she mumbled her thanks around a mouthful of rice. With my own bowl in hand I went to the armchair in the opposite corner of the room. My drink was already nearby, too, a non-alcoholic cider with ice still bouncing on the liquid's surface. I only ever bought wine when I knew Rebecca was visiting. More and more over the years, I'd found that drinking – either alone or in company – brought out a deep ache of melancholy in me that was a foe I didn't think worth inviting in too often.

'This is bloody delicious.'

I laughed. 'Thank you, it's a new recipe.'

'Honestly, that cookbook you wrote was worth its weight.'

I had been one of two ghostwriters on a cookbook project that was distributed by my agency just before I moved here. They had given us a list of meal types that needed to be included, along with a generous expenditure budget for actually making those meals ahead of writing their recipes down. It had been a fun project to spend time with – and my cooking had improved considerably over the course of it, too.

'What did the boys think of the cottage pie?'

'They didn't come.' I forked in a mouthful of rice. 'They were busy.'

'Both of them?'

'Mm,' I mumbled in answer. Rebecca would not stand for her children cancelling how I stood for mine doing it. Though the lives of my boys and the lives of her two boys and a girl had been very different. 'You know how things are for them–' she didn't, of course, not even their partners could know, '–and the cottage pie can be remade another night. It really doesn't matter too much.'

'You give them more slack than they deserve. When did you last see them?'

I tried to place the visit. 'Two months or so.'

'*Two?* Jesus, my Louise is round every week at the minute.'

Louise was five months pregnant. She was moving through that period of the gestation process where she was brutally angry with her husband for not having to share in her physical discomfort and as such, she was confiding in the only woman who might understand her literal and emotional pain: her mother. I sometimes wished I'd had girls. But given the upbringing the boys had to suffer through, I wasn't altogether sure that having had girls would have necessarily made a difference to the contact I had with my children now.

'Have they rescheduled?'

'I've got a lot of work on at the moment. I told them both that we should try to arrange something for when this project is out of the way.' I didn't have any more work on than usual; I just knew Rebecca would pull out a hearty lecture if I'd admitted that no, they hadn't rescheduled. During their rehearsed conversations about not being able to make dinner for X, Y and Z reasons, neither of them had thought to even mention the possibility of re-making the plans they had called to cancel. I thought I'd raised them better than that, and I had to wonder whether they'd be so flippant with their friends. Though I couldn't decide whether it would comfort or disappoint me to know.

Rebecca made a face.

'Is there something wrong with the food?'

'No, silly, there's something wrong with those boys of yours.'

'Rebecca...' I cautioned.

She held up one hand in mock surrender, the other still clutching her bowl. 'I know better than to poke the bear. I just think that after you made the effort, they could have made the effort. Besides, what happened to all those ingredients? What a waste, I'll bet.'

I bunched my lips up at one side before tucking into a mouthful of rice.

'You took it to the bloody food shelter, didn't you?'

A laugh hiccupped out of me. 'Yes, I took it to the bloody shelter,' I answered, my tone a mock of hers. 'It's for a good cause, Rebecca. You should try coming with me one evening a week. You might be surprised at how much you enjoy it when you're actually there, meeting new people, helping them.'

She rolled her eyes. 'Please. I serve dinner to my Tommy every night already and there is *nothing* gratifying about it.' Tommy was Rebecca's husband; they'd been married for thirty-nine years. Rebecca was hardly eighteen when they ran away and tied the knot and told their disapproving parents after the fact.

'Well, the offer is there.'

'I tell you what,' she paused mid-sentence for a sip of her wine, 'I'll come to the food shelter with you when you agree to come to a Zumba class with me.'

I shifted rice grains around and avoided eye contact. 'That's not a fair deal.'

Rebecca laughed. There was still a trace of ex-smoker in the sound even though she told me it had been years since she'd had a cigarette. I sometimes wondered whether that was true. 'You're right, it isn't a fair deal. Bloody food shelter.'

'That isn't what I meant and you well know–'

'Maggie, come on. You work at that laptop all day and I know, I know,' she cut off my protest before I could let it take root, 'you try to have your lunchtime walks, I *know*. But you're hunched up at that laptop and you're staring at that screen. Don't you think a bit of exercise would do you good? And it's a social thing, too! It isn't just about moving and dancing. We all have a right laugh.'

It had been a long time since I'd had a 'right laugh'. It was on my list of restrictions.

'I'll think about it,' I lied.

'And I'll think about the food shelter,' Rebecca lied back.

While we finished our respective bowls of food Rebecca held the conversation steady with snippets of pregnancy bliss. Louise was so big and the baby so big and both so healthy and– The boys had both explicitly told me they didn't want children. I couldn't blame them. The parenting model they'd been exposed to can't have instilled much faith in them about the process of creating and raising a family. Their father and I did okay for the first ten years apiece but their teenage years were tainted, I knew, and there was nothing that could ease the distortions and smudges around those years in their lives.

'Don't you think that's the sweetest thing?'

I snapped back into the room. 'It certainly sounds it.'

'Honestly, Mags, that was delicious.' She rested her bowl on top of the one that had held prawn crackers earlier. 'You'll have to come over to mine one evening, migrate back and I'll cook for you. We'll throw Tommy out somewhere. I'll up his allowance and he can have an extra night at the pub.' She rolled her eyes as though she minded being the money-handler of their home but I knew that she didn't, in the same way that Tommy didn't mind being the breadwinner still. He was still happy to come home covered in grime and grit and the stink of highway maintenance. I'd only met him a handful of times, but that was the image I carried of him. I couldn't picture him clean-cut, or in jeans that didn't have stains and puncture marks on them.

'Think about coming back for the night?' she pushed when I didn't answer.

I hadn't been back to the town where Rebecca and I had met since I fled from there the first time: my house sold for less than its market value; my personal belongings temporarily thrown in a storage locker. It hadn't been the most pleasant of goodbyes – and I hadn't told Rebecca I was leaving until the day after I was gone.

I mumbled in agreement and rested my empty bowl on the side table. My cider glass had left a spill of condensation across the table's surface, even though I'd used a coaster. 'I'll think about it, and I'll think about Zumba. But for now, I'd like to think about pudding.'

'Pudding too?' she asked with a child's excitement.

'Pineapple upside-down cake.'

Rebecca made an appreciative gasp. 'Honestly, Maggie, how some man hasn't snapped you up since the divorce I'll never know.'

Of course, Rebecca couldn't know that I was still cleaning wounds left over from that first snap from a man. I bathed them in salt water every morning and dressed them fresh, knitted together stitches when necessary and took painkillers on the worst of days. They weren't visible lesions but they were there; under the surface, carved into the core. If another man had ever come close enough to learn me, he likely would have felt my first husband's etchings like braille: small warnings from our marriage; my many shortfalls as a wife.

I served her cake with double cream and I asked to know more about Louise.

FOUR

I walked to Sarah's. The weather was terrible, but somehow that gave me greater motivation to leave the car at home and to brave the elements. It was raining, but it brought with it that autumnal sting; the early bite of cold that acts as a prologue to a harsh winter. There were already early predictions that October and November would bring with them deep frosts and feet of snow. Though given that the weather for this day hadn't meant to be rain at all, but sunny spells with gentle winds, I wasn't yet willing to subscribe to the idea of a winter-long hibernation. Or rather, I likely was ready to subscribe to that idea, but not because of anything to do with the weather itself.

Despite the promise of the day, I was wearing my winter coat already. My hood was pulled tight around my face with a fur trim that obscured my sightline, and I had paired it with an umbrella. The efforts felt somewhat wasted, though, as the rain slowly worked through the bottom halves of my clothing; coat and jeans both, with my black pumps soon soaked through by puddles and the backsplash that crept onto the pavement, thanks to careless drivers who didn't mind soaking pedestrians on their travels. Not that there were many other walkers about. I bumped into two others, literally, owing to my limited view of the world, but both of them hurried past me before I could mumble my apologies. I realised then that 'Sorry' had been the first word I had said aloud that day, which felt telling.

Sarah answered my email quickly. I had sat down at my kitchen table with the best of intentions to get work done. But after staring at the clock and date in the bottom-right corner of the screen, for what turned out to be seven minutes, I thought company other than my own might be a better remedy to the day. She'd said she had a busy day ahead but of course she'd like to see me, if I could pop over mid-morning then she had a little free time then. I looked hard into that 'of course' to check for signs of sincerity or falsity. It could be so difficult to tell, when it came to written communications over spoken ones; that bit easier, to lie in writing rather than verbally. Strange, really, considering that long term, one could be so much more damning than the other. In the end, though, my desire for company had won out over my paranoia that Sarah was feigning interest in spending time with me. And I had managed to work my way through to nearly mid-morning, before leaving for this battle against rain and drivers.

I rang the bell to Sarah's building and tried to origami as much of myself as I could under the shelter of her doorway while I waited for the abrupt burst of noise that would signal the door unlocking. While I waited, I listed all of the things I needed to do that day. It was a list that became so overwhelming I began to wonder whether this hour away from work was a luxury I could afford at all. But then I felt the rattle of an acorn around my skull, the clink of it hitting one side and then the other. Perhaps it wasn't an acorn at all, but rather a steel marble lost inside the shell of an old pinball machine. *Yes,* I thought then, *yes, I need this time away.*

The door opened, giving me cause to step back, and there

Sarah was with a wide and seemingly authentic smile. 'I hit the buzzer to let you in.'

'Oh.' I shook my head and felt the steel marble move. 'I'm sorry, I...'

'Miles away?' She stepped aside to let me into the building. 'Come on in. I've got a gas fire going in my room this morning so those wet clothes are in luck.'

'Thank you.'

After a walk made up of inconsiderate drivers, Sarah's kindness felt greater to me than it perhaps was in reality. I thanked her another two times as I unbuttoned my coat and draped it on the floor in front of the heater. Then began the cliché and oftentimes useless process of rubbing my hands together for a few seconds before putting them in front of the heater for a few seconds and repeating, as though the actions, coupled, would remedy the cold that had seeded into my bones on the walk.

Rain thrashed against the windows of the old building and I wondered whether a taxi home might be a wiser decision, over tackling the pavements that would no doubt be waterlogged if this kept up. The drains around here were in desperate need of cleaning, fallen leaves had clogged their arteries already in nature's yearly shed, but no one seemed in a rush for that upkeep. I added 'email council' to my list of things to do later in the day.

'This'll warm you up.' Sarah stepped back into the room with two steaming mugs. She knew how I took my coffee without asking, which felt like another kindness. There weren't many people who knew me that well anymore. 'Get yourself settled on the sofa.'

I did as I was told. The plush of Sarah's sofa cushioned in around me. I ran my palms over the soft fabric before grabbing at a pillow to position on my lap. I took the mug of coffee when it was offered and balanced it between my hands. The heat of it was too much and the more sensible thing would have been to put it on the table to rest into a manageable temperature, but I was worried that that may seem like ingratitude. I was worried, too, that I would inevitably forget to drink it once Sarah and I began setting the world right with our chatter, which would have been a greater show of ingratitude still. So instead I cradled the heat and let it course through my joints until they ached with it.

Sarah dropped down on the sofa opposite me, with the heaviness that comes with landing on your own furniture.

'How have you been?' and 'How are you?' rushed out of us both at the same time, and the questions chipped away at any ice in the room. 'You first,' Sarah said, reaching forwards for her drink, and then she nestled back against the sofa as though making herself comfortable for a monologue. I wasn't sure I had that much to say.

Though when I eventually glanced at the clock I found I'd spent nearly twenty minutes talking to her about the recipe for that lentil cottage pie. Sarah seemed interested though. Halfway through she even stood up to grab a sheet of scrap paper and a pen so she could note down some details of the ingredients. Every now and then she made appreciative noises as though a portion had been set down in front of her. There was a Tupperware container of it in the freezer still that I'd kept for this week. I should have brought it.

'Did it bother you that the boys didn't visit?'

My head jerked back as though I were physically recoiling from the question. I had expected something about measurements, or how long to soak lentils for. 'No more than it usually bothers me when they cancel.'

Sarah's mouth tugged downwards either side; she was

resisting a frown, I thought. 'Did they give you reasons for not coming?'

'They said they were too busy.'

'And you didn't ask what they were busy with?'

I shook my head. 'I didn't want to pry.'

'Hm.' She set the scrap paper on the table and dropped the pen next to it. 'Maggie, why did you ask to see me today?'

It was, I suppose, a fair question. My meetings with Sarah were only semi-regular now, having disintegrated to something I arranged on an as-needed basis. Given that I had emailed at such an early hour that it could have been deemed antisocial by some, she was within her rights to assume there was something specific that I wanted to talk about. There probably was, too, I just hadn't realised it yet.

'I don't think I wanted to talk about the boys,' I answered. I thought process of elimination may get me closer to the root of the cause. *How long have I* actually *been talking about cooking?* I glanced at the clock and saw that it had leapt forward another twenty minutes from the last time I'd checked. 'I'm sorry if I'm wasting your time.'

She held up a hand and shook her head. 'You couldn't if you tried.'

'I'm sure that's not true.' I sipped at my coffee, which was now so cold that I had to swallow it with a wince. 'I've been thinking about my ex-husband a lot,' I admitted, though I spoke into the hollow space of my cup.

'I see.'

'Today would have been our anniversary.'

When I was a child we'd had a family cat called Mittens. I suppose I'd been allowed to name her. Mum hadn't wanted the responsibility of a cat at all, but Dad and I had promised that she would be more ours than Mum's. Mittens, perceptive creature that she was, would often come strolling into the living room while we were having family time, our empty dinner plates still balanced on our knees while we were all waiting for an interval in whatever soap opera Mum happened to have encouraged Dad and I into watching. My sister must have been there, too, though I could never place her in these memories. Mittens would position herself directly in front of Mum and start by arching her back. Then, like a teenage girl regretful of her decision to eat cake with friends, Mittens would huff and heave and make herself gag, until a wretched and soaked furball emerged from her, landing at Mum's feet like an offering. Mum would wail until Dad or I intervened to remove the offending article, and shoo Mittens back out of the room with a tap on her behind, too, if we'd managed to swipe at her.

That's how I imagined my admission: a wretched and soaked thing at Sarah's feet.

'Is that why you've been thinking of him, more so than usual?' she asked.

No. I shook my head in answer. 'I don't think so. I think–' I tried to swallow the false start before I heaved the sentence out in full. In the background, somewhere, I half-heard Sarah telling me to take my time. 'I think I've been thinking about him because I have this strange, strange feeling,' I paused as though that were the complete thought before forcing out the end, 'this strange feeling that something is going to happen to him soon.'

FIVE

The feeling was right, but its direction was wrong.

It had been a long day of browsing work assignments. The agency had sent through several potential jobs that I might like. After two hours of drawing a shortlist from them all, I realised that my working week would need to grow to sixty hours if not more to even begin catering to the demands of blog posts, academic blurbs, and the many other tasks that I had put into this alleged shortlist that, on reflection, was perhaps not that short. I would need to revise the shortlist, which I guessed would take at least another coffee.

I paced the kitchen while the kettle boiled. The garden still needed tending to; that was another list. I hadn't drafted that one in order of importance, though, only in order of need or want; which is to say, the jobs I believed I could tackle the easiest without hiring help or asking for it from my sons, neither of which were prospects that I felt especially warm towards, were at the top of the list. There was ivy beginning to climb across the boundary of my fencing, though, and kind as my neighbours were – or at least they seemed to be, from the times I'd viewed them through my living-room window while they were carrying their shopping bags in, or jostling with their children on the front lawn – I didn't imagine they'd care much for the encroachment of a green creature that looked to be somehow piercing holes through the fencing. *That'll need to be dealt with*, I thought as I poured water into my mug and watched as the coffee granules stained the colour of it. That's when the front doorbell rang.

I checked the clock on the wall, then my watch, as though to corroborate the initial time. It was hardly the end of the working day, not for anyone willing to put a full day's work in at least. So on the walk from one side of downstairs to the other I weighed up whether this was more likely to be a charity worker or a door-to-door salesperson.

Oh, I realised when the door was only half-open, *neither*.

Kitsell and Thompson were both so much older than they had been when this had all started. Though I imagined they thought the same of me, too. When we'd first met, I still had naturally blonde hair, only pulled through with strands of silver; the silver had since overtaken my head, and I had long ago stopped bothering with the hassle of trying to tame its natural frizz. I no longer wore tight-fitting jeans but loose-fit ones instead; in part because time changes us all and in part because my weight had fluctuated so much over the years, it was impossible to tell what size I might need. Kitsell appeared to have had a similar problem, though his weight was considerably greater than when I'd last seen him. He boasted a middle-aged paunch over the lip of his trousers that spelled a happy and content life. Thompson had always been the more athletic one of the two; even now, in his casual dress, it was easy to see the outline of a runner's physique, trainers rather than shoes as though he were ready to run at any minute. But given the job they were likely here for, I thought perhaps that might be exactly how he felt.

The three of us swapped awkward smiles, unsure of how to greet each other. Inwardly, though, one small thought chased its tail around my head; a squirrel trying to catch the elusive acorn: *It's happened then. He's finally died.*

'Maggie,' Thompson set a foot on the proverbial ice and held out his hand, 'good to see you.'

'Of course, of course.' It sounded like I was agreeing, but the unsettled part of me – which, admittedly, was the more dominant part of me on any given day, never mind in the face of two retired detectives – completely forgot to take his hand. Instead, I only sidestepped to give them an avenue into the house. 'Please, do come in.'

Kitsell's stomach brushed against me as he shuffled past, a thin-lipped smile fixed in place. The pair of them lingered in the hallway then, and I remembered that they didn't yet know this home. They had only seen the first three or four, after. When the case had a thick line drawn underneath it there was never a reason for them to visit.

'If you go straight ahead, we can sit in the kitchen.' I didn't mind them seeing the scuttle of work papers on the table. I liked for them to think I was busy. 'I've just boiled the kettle, if either of you want a drink?'

'I'll take a coffee, please, Maggie,' Kitsell answered. Thompson only shook his head.

'Sit anywhere, please,' I gestured to the table, 'don't mind the clutter.'

Thompson eyed the papers carefully as he sat down, as though inspecting a cadaver rather than a body of work. 'You're keeping busy,' he said then.

'I'm trying to.' I grabbed a cup from the cupboard ahead of me and fixed Kitsell his coffee. I could still remember how he took it. And that's when it erupted out of me, like acid reflux that I couldn't hold down. 'He's died then.'

There was a long pause before Kitsell answered. 'No, actually.'

'More to the pity,' Thompson added under his breath. But nowhere near quiet enough for myself or Kitsell to miss it; evidenced by the cutting look I saw one man shoot the other as I turned around. 'No, he hasn't,' Thompson carried on then in a notably more professional tone, 'but the doctors are saying it won't be long.'

'I see.' I put Kitsell's coffee down on top of a to-do list I couldn't remember writing, before taking my own lukewarm drink to my seat. I closed my laptop and rested my mug on top of it. 'Then to what do I owe the pleasure?'

Kitsell cleared his throat. 'Edward is working with the police at the moment, Maggie, to provide information on the case that we were unable to get the first time around.'

'On the missing girls,' Thompson added, in case I was in any doubt about what they were referring to. 'Something about wanting to clear his conscience before he... passes.'

'That's good of him,' I answered, my tone deadpan. 'Does that mean you have questions– Are there things I can be helping with?'

I had tried so hard to help the first time around. But there's only so much information you can provide when the police are trying to explain to you that your husband is a serial murderer – and you are trying to explain to them that of course he can't be.

'In a fashion,' Kitsell said, taking over. He sipped his drink before continuing. 'Edward has made some requests–'

'Demands.'

Kitsell side-eyed his partner. 'Edward has made some requests that he would like met, ahead of sharing– Well, ahead of telling us anything about the girls and what happened to them, and most importantly where the last victim– Where Lucy is.'

I swallowed hard and felt the bulge of an acorn in my throat. 'Right.'

'One of his requests, Maggie, is that– Well, one of the requests is that you visit him.'

'That's not technically true,' Thompson chimed, sounding deeply unimpressed. 'One of the requests is that instead of talking to us, he be allowed to talk to you.'

I narrowed my eyes to try to find meaning underneath, in between, behind the words. 'I'm not sure I...'

'He wants to confess to you, Maggie,' Thompson snapped. The plain English wasn't any easier to understand. 'He wants for you to be the one he speaks to, about everything.'

Before my husband was my husband, he was only a teenage boy in the playground. We'd been from opposing schools; me at the all-girls academy, him at the all-boys. It was an exercise in trust that our schoolteachers allowed us to mix during break-times, a way of collapsing the literal walls between us all. He had wanted to speak to me then but hadn't quite had the courage for it. Instead, he'd sent a friend of his across to me, where I lingered with my group of girlfriends. Only the friend had been so nervous himself that he hadn't managed to verbally deliver the message, and had handed over a hastily written note that read: *Edward would really like to speak to you*. I wondered whether my husband thought I would remember those beginnings, whether he was counting on it.

I forced another swallow; though this one felt like it might choke me. 'No.'

Kitsell glanced at Thompson, who shrugged. 'Just... no?' Kitsell asked.

'Maggie, I understand this is a heinous bullshit thing of him to ask you–'

'No,' I interrupted Thompson, who seemed to be speaking under the misguided belief that taking a softer tone with me would help me to change my mind. 'I'm not comfortable doing it. I'm afraid you'll have to barter something else for his penance.' I stood from the table then in an uncharacteristically rude attempt at ceasing the conversation altogether. 'If my husband is so desperate to repent while he still can, might I suggest getting the man a priest?'

'That, I do understand.' Thompson stood and held out his hand again. This time I took it with an abrupt and singular shake. 'I'm not sure I could break for the bastard either.'

'Clive,' Kitsell cautioned. 'Of course, we understand it's a great ask.' He stood, leaving his half-sipped coffee abandoned in the centre of a to-do list that I now had no inclination or interest in caring for. I couldn't even remember what set of jobs it related to – and things had been so organised before they arrived. 'Maggie, if you do change your mind, look,' he handed over a scrap of paper with his phone number written on it, 'will you call me, please?'

I took note of the fact that it was a Post-it note with the glue ridge folded down on it. It was no longer a business card with the police station's emblem in the corner. 'I won't.'

He dropped the paper on the table. 'Understood.'

'We'll see ourselves out.' Thompson squeezed my shoulder as he walked by. 'Despite the circumstances, it was good to see you, Maggie.'

'You take care now,' Kitsell added, already in the doorway of the kitchen.

I had no pleasant goodbyes to offer either of them. I only managed to hold myself upright long enough for the front door to slam, before collapsing back onto the chair behind me. It felt as though a small hurricane had swept through my innards. My breath came in jagged bursts, sails gagging for air against a turbulent sea wind. I thought that when they came it would be when it had happened. I imagined sullen expressions hiding quiet relief that the man they caught had finally got the comeuppance he deserved. But of course, that wouldn't be the case; of course, it would be Edward again asking for something he knew I couldn't give. There had been certain things I had compromised on, always: a weekend away for work despite my own plans; an evening with colleagues he knew I couldn't stand; caring for his ailing mother after the cancer diagnosis. But then, there had been compromises I couldn't make, too: namely, an alibi for nights when I had known that no, he was not with me; no, I hadn't known exactly where he was.

Now, this.

But I could not, would not, bend, I thought as I grabbed at the edge of the table to anchor myself. I could not, would not, speak to my husband. I hadn't – not since the police had told me about the women. All nine of them.

SIX

It was two days later when I decided to tend to and chop at the garden. I didn't know the names of the remaining flowers, only knew how their colours paired together; which ones would make worthy bedfellows for a small bouquet. I kept them in a pint glass filled with water, balanced in the kitchen sink. There had to be ribbon in the house somewhere, but I couldn't find it for looking. So instead of being bound together with a neat bow they were held tight by a brown elastic band that I thought I'd perhaps tightened around the waists of the flower stems one too many times. But at least they would hold well. I left them waiting while I finished off the day's work, writing bids for new contracts and otherwise busying myself, under the pretence that there wasn't a nest of hornets living behind my eyes. I had managed five hours' sleep across two nights since Kitsell and Thompson had been, though I couldn't work out whether it was worry or a guilty conscience keeping me awake.

I checked my phone again in case Bernie had returned my call and I'd somehow missed it – but no. My sister and I had had a strained relationship since Edward and I became serious. It hadn't been anything to do with what he did; her dislike of him stretched back years before that. My parents – both passed now, one having followed the other such is so often the way with older couples – had never warmed to him either, though they'd managed enough pleasantries to get us through birthdays, Christmases and the few other family gatherings over the years. They'd also come to mine and Edward's wedding – unlike Bernie, who had only RSVP'd "No". I remembered how she'd underlined the box, as though merely placing a tick inside of it hadn't been a definitive enough rejection. When he'd been arrested, investigated, found guilty of it all, my parents had been as supportive as Mum's failing health allowed them to be. They offered to take the boys whenever I needed the space – or whenever I needed to move us all to a different location in the dead of night, while the reporters were resting. They offered a roof over my head, too, though I'd turned down the offer, owing to the fact that life was already a media circus for me and the boys by then, and the last thing the situation called for was a worsening of that. I'd wanted to keep my family as far away from the amateur dramatics of it all as I could. Bernie's support had been limited by comparison. Once she'd got her spite out of her system – with several renditions of 'I told you so' in varying forms – she visited me only once and, finding the reporters too close to bloodhounds for her liking, had lessened her support to weekly phone calls instead. Since Mum and Dad had passed away, we hadn't even managed that much.

Monthly phone calls was closer to our connection now, though they were still strained and awkward. We would limp through fifteen minutes of asking how each other's children were before saying we'd catch up soon. It had only been two weeks since we'd last spoken, so we weren't due for a check-in. After two days of rolling around the house alone, though, she had been the only person I could think to call. Which said everything there was to know about my life now, I thought. It wasn't that I didn't have friends; only that none of them knew, none of them could know, that Maggie wasn't my real name, that so many reporters had once known me as Linda, that Edward O'Connor, the man responsible for the deaths of at least nine young women, was my husband.

I swallowed a mouthful of cold coffee, collected my phone from the table, and called Bernie again. It rang out three times and I braced my core for the automated answer-machine voice to kick in. There was a spasm in my lower gut when Bernie's curt tone came down the line instead.

'I was going to leave a message,' I said in place of a hello.

'Well, now you don't have to. Is everything okay?'

'I called, a day or so ago.'

'I've been busy. Is everything okay?' She sounded impatient, bored with me already, and I could have doubled over with discomfort against her obvious disinterest.

'I was wondering whether I could pop over and see you this week.'

There was a long pause before she answered. 'Has something happened?'

'Yes. But I'd like to talk about it in person, if you have the time?' I realised how needy, how pleading I sounded, but this human connection was all I had to cling to when it came to matters of my husband. *Ex-husband*, I corrected. But of course, as far as anyone else was concerned, when it came to matters of Edward O'Connor I would always be The Wife. 'I understand if you're busy.'

'It's a little late in the day now.'

It was hardly outside of working hours even, but I mumbled in agreement all the same. 'Perhaps I could come over tomorrow?'

'In the daytime?'

'Of course.'

Bernie was on her second marriage. The girls' father had passed away in a car accident when they were barely old enough to walk unaided; neither of them had living memories of him, which was a truth that broke my heart. We were a family that had known too much death. Now, I could only visit when Jonathan – Bernie's second husband – was out of the house. He didn't know that I existed. Bernie had wanted something untarnished, she said, and I had understood that all too well.

'If you come over at about lunchtime, I'll fix us something.' It was an uncharacteristically kind offer, and I was immediately suspicious. 'If you'd rather not eat here, that's also fine, I was only–'

'No, no, that would be lovely, thank you.'

'I'll see you at about lunchtime tomorrow.'

'I'll see you then.'

Bernie ended the call without a goodbye, which felt much more in character for her.

I eyed the flowers in the sink still before checking the time again. It wasn't late enough in the day to leave. Besides which, even if I braved it during daylight hours the work traffic between here and Westland Woods would be a nightmare. I decided to brew another coffee and make a cheese sandwich, and work beyond my usual time. There was certainly enough to get through to warrant it. I had written another one thousand words and whittled my sandwich down to its crusts and dark had fallen outside. And I decided it was probably safe, by then, for me to leave.

Edward and I had taken the boys to Westland Woods habitually when they were children. It was a wild and beautiful landscape of overgrown trees and shrubbery. There was a child's paradise of monkey bars and seesaws situated right in the centre of it, too; the gooey, exciting core that we arrived at once we'd all battled through the surrounding mess. No matter the time of year we somehow always came home with shoes caked of mud and clothes that needed a hot wash. Edward and I would sit with our packed lunches while the boys exhausted themselves, intermittently running back to us to grab their packets of raisins, chew the occasional bite of sandwich, rush away with half a banana in hand, while he and I quietly watched this beautiful life we had made together.

The woods used to be on our doorstep; a mere fifteen-minute drive away. Now, it took me nearly two hours even with little traffic on the roads. I had moved so far away, each house a greater distance than the last, as though I could outrun the ghosts of this life by changing my postcode enough times. And yet I still couldn't outrun Edward, moved from one prison to another then another during his sentence, he was practically on my doorstep now; a dangerous proximity.

The women weren't all from our local area, but somehow they found their way there. One had been visiting a friend when Edward met her. Another had been out of the town limits entirely, but he had chosen to bring her home. The other seven had been snatched from within the town's boundaries; a big enough area code for the girls to not all know each other, but a small enough circumference for the police to have decided they were searching for a local man. I could remember the news reports too well; how they were always looking for a man and never a woman. I had commented to Edward about it once, how it was always the way; I could remember his answer still, too: 'It's always some angry man, isn't it?' He'd been sitting at our kitchen table reading the morning paper at the time.

A road sign alerted me that the woods were only three more miles away, and I felt a breath catch in my throat when I realised how close I was to it all. It wouldn't have surprised me if the spectre of a young woman had stepped out from a roadside hedge and started to wave her arms, encouraging me to turn around. *Because I don't belong here,* I thought, though I tried to shoo the idea away. I didn't come here often, but this wasn't my first visit since.

I pulled into the woodland car park and stalled the car before I could extinguish the engine properly. The sound of it dying seemed to echo out. I imagined it disturbing wildlife for miles.

The flowers were resting on the passenger seat. I snatched at them and opened my door before I could talk myself out of the plan. My breathing was already coming in jagged bursts; the labouring that a person sometimes feels when breathing against cold air, though the weather hadn't yet cooled enough to justify it, despite the time of year. As I started to tread through the outskirts of the woods I felt the soft earth giving way one footstep at a time. I imagined another spectre then, reaching up through the ground to pull me into it, chased by a chanting of 'Why me? Why us? Why not you?' Though the answer to that was simple: I hadn't been Edward's type.

He had chosen young women, hardly out of their teens. They were young enough to trust an older man; old enough that their families didn't immediately realise they were missing. There were two who weren't reported missing at all; no one had noticed they were gone until they were found, and my heart had always ached a little more for those than the others.

The garden was a small and cordoned off space, not as far into the grounds as the play area was. The council had planted evergreens in a small border. But every time I had been here the space had always been laden with flowers. My own small offering seemed meagre in comparison to the ones resting here now: large gatherings of white roses; lilies that would never fully bloom out of water. I knocked my legs into autopilot to resist the urge of stopping to read the notes and cards that had been left, too. There would be some here from their mothers and fathers, and years ago I had promised myself that I would give up the torture of reading any scriptures of their grief – though perhaps I deserved to. Instead of stopping, I coursed to the centre of the space where the memorial plaque stood. It was a squat structure with a gold plate at its top, engraved and clearly tended to regularly. Even in this darkness, the women's names were clear.

I rested the small bundle of flowers at the base of the stand and, as was my new habit when visiting, I read each entry of the nine-strong list: Ella; Abigail; Isla; Hannah; Sophie; Lucy; Ruby; Chloe and Grace. But it was the inscription that came after this that caused a small and strangled animal sound to tumble out of me. There, beneath their names in perfect cursive: '*And for the others lost, and never found.*'

Lucy's body was never recovered, even though they'd scoured the woods for her. She was a late edition to Edward's set, a presumed victim though he would never grant the family the certainty of knowing what truly happened to her. Kitsell and Thompson had never given up hope of finding her and I knew it had been that hope, and their grit, that had brought them to my door days ago. That, and the other women – lost, but not found.

Because, of course, everyone had always known how likely it was that there had been more than just nine.

SEVEN

A stranger could be forgiven for thinking that Bernie didn't have children. Admittedly, the girls hadn't lived with her for some time. Nevertheless, there were no signs of them at all around the house. The only framed photographs that remained pinned to the walls were ones of her and Jonathan, enjoying their many travels around the world. He was a high-powered something in the tech industry. All I knew for certain was that he worked with computers, and judging from the size and condition of their house, and the frequency of their holidays, it appeared that he did that work particularly well. Bernie didn't have to work, nor was she one of those women who chose to work, despite her husband covering their financial outgoings. She let Jonathan take care of the comings and goings with money while she tended to their home; an occupation that seemed stranger still given that all that needed tending to was housework, which was minimal without the patter of offspring to cause too much of a mess. I wondered how many hours a day she must spend cleaning, or sitting perhaps, and waiting for her husband to come home. She'd sounded busy when I called her yesterday and I thought I must have caught her polishing the kitchen floor, or some other urgent business. Urgency, of course, being a relative term.

Bernie asked me to take my shoes off in the entryway. 'We've just had the carpets deep cleaned,' she explained, hurrying down the corridor toward the kitchen. 'You can just make yourself at home,' she said over her shoulder. My idea of making myself at home meant that I was padding barefoot around her living room, inspecting pictures of trips I didn't know she'd taken. I felt an all too familiar tug; a loose rope knotted around something inside me, handed to a toddler and yanked. It came often, and for a multitude of reasons. Today, I thought it must be longing – though for what, I was unsure.

'That was a cruise we went on earlier in the year.'

I shot upright as though I'd been caught inspecting something I shouldn't.

'It was lovely just to get away from things.'

Bernie wandered into the room, dropped herself into a worn armchair and pulled her legs up beneath her. I was desperate to ask what "things" it was that her and Jonathan needed to get away from.

'Please, sit,' she gestured to the sofa in front of her. 'I'm making quiche but it'll be another thirty minutes or so. I'm sorry, I got my timings all off for when you'd be here.'

I apologised twice as I sat down. We'd agreed on lunchtime but it had always felt especially vague to me: breakfast time, lunchtime and so on. With everyone's bodies operating on a different time schedule for needing food, and having time to eat food, I was never sure what window of time I was operating within when a mealtime had been the basis for a clock.

'You didn't need to go to any trouble, with food.'

She flashed me a thin smile. 'I didn't.'

'Well, thank you all the same.'

The same awkward silence characteristic of mine and my sister's time together settled over us then. In the end, I fractured the quiet by asking about the girls. They were doing well, she said. The youngest working abroad and the eldest working down in London; both were healthy, happy. Neither of them were especially interested in children, and it struck me as interesting that she felt the need to mention that. I wondered how many of her friends must ask whether she was a grandmother yet, whether she was desperate to be. It was a universally accepted area of conversation among women, I'd found. Though for a long time I hadn't been close enough to anyone for them to pry into such intimate details.

'How are the boys?'

'They're well. They were over for dinner the other night actually,' I lied. I didn't particularly like to fabricate these things, but Bernie made me feel a deep need to. 'They're working hard, but it was nice to spend some time with them.'

'What did you have?'

'I'm sorry?'

'To eat,' she clarified. 'What did you have to eat?'

'Oh, lentil cottage pie.' When I'd decided on that meal plan for the dinner that didn't happen, I hadn't imagined I would spend quite so much of my time talking about the recipe for that damn cottage pie in the days after. But soon I found myself divulging the intricacies of the ingredients to her, in parrot fashion to how I'd shared them with Sarah.

Bernie flashed that same thin smile. 'Jonathan doesn't like lentils.'

'Ah. Well, you could swap the lentils for anything I suppose.'

'Mm,' she murmured in a way that suggested I was in fact completely wrong. 'Do you want to eat at the table?'

'Oh, I'm happy wherever.'

'We'll eat at the table then. Do you want to get yourself settled?'

The living room and dining room in Bernie's house was open-plan. The table she'd been referring to was at the other end of the room, just beyond a sideboard partition that boasted yet more photographs of her worldly existence. I took a seat that meant I could look into the garden and I tried to draft a list of jobs that needed completing out there. I was dumbstruck to find there were none, though, and I wondered whether that was something Jonathan tended to, or whether that fell to Bernie as well.

She brought through a tray with small plates, a large plate boasting the entire quiche, and a bowl of salad. 'I'll just get some water,' she said before disappearing again into the kitchen. The sound of her humming drifted through the open hatch that sat in the centre of the wall between the rooms. 'Help yourself.' She set a jug of water down in front of me, ice cubes knocking together in percussion, and placed two glasses on the table, too. I was glad to have something to busy myself with.

Again, that familiar silence fell over us; a pall covering the room. Bernie dished up neat slices of quiche for us both and told me to help myself to the salad. I was about to busy myself further with the act of eating – I couldn't remember having had anything beyond a cheese sandwich in the days since the detectives' visit – when Bernie took her turn in breaking the quiet.

'So what's the matter?'

My head shot up. 'Why do you assume something is the matter?'

'We're not due for a call,' she tucked a cluster of mixed leaves into her mouth and spoke around them, 'and you seldom ask whether you can come to the house.' A piece of red onion escaped the corner of her mouth and she tucked it back in with a nail that looked false. That was new.

'Edward has asked to see me.'

Bernie's eyes widened and she coughed with such gusto that she was soon slamming a balled fist against her chest. I reached across to pour and pass her a glass of water. Her eyes were watering by then. She managed two sips and soon the coughing settled.

Even now, I wasn't sure what I thought I would gain from having told her. I was married to the idea of not seeing him at all, not winding myself into this deathbed story-time. And yet... It occurred to me I may have told her knowing that her disapproval would cement my decision. It was a validation I didn't know I needed. But who better to provide it than my judgemental older sister?

'Why?' she eventually asked.

'He's going to die soon, and there are confessions he wants to share.'

'And he has to share them with you?'

'That's one of his demands.'

'Of course it is.' She turned her attention back to eating. She had chewed through a mouthful of quiche before she spoke again. 'These confessions, they're about the deaths?'

I nodded. 'I can't think what else they'd be about.'

'That girl's body?'

'Lucy,' I snapped, 'her name was Lucy.'

'Okay. Lucy's body.'

'I don't know, Bernie.' I sagged in my seat. It had only been a handful of questions, but it felt very much as though they'd punctured me. 'I told the police I wouldn't do it.'

She loaded up another forkful of quiche and mixed leaves. 'I see.'

I'd suddenly lost my appetite. But I knew it would be

perceived as ingratitude, so I forked into the quiche and tucked away a mouthful. I slow-chewed then, imagining it were something bearable – rather than something that had the texture of fresh ash. I cut into it with my teeth over and over until the pastry disintegrated into mulch.

'Have you spoken to the boys about it?'

I shook my head and forced a swallow. 'No. I said no as soon as I was asked and that's all there is to it.'

'That isn't true,' she answered, and she noticed my brow furrow. 'If that was all there was to this then you wouldn't have wandered into my home with this little announcement.' She wiped her mouth on a brilliant-white napkin and took a sip of water. 'You should talk to the boys before you decide to do it.'

'Bernie I told you I said–'

'This is the last decent thing you can do for those girls, for their *parents*.' She leaned on the word so heavily that I worried she might tumble through it. 'Talk to the boys, call the detectives, get it over with. You've spent years administering half-hearted penance for not doing something sooner,' she speared another piece of quiche and I felt the prongs in my stomach, 'now's your chance to do something right in it all.'

Thirty minutes later Bernie saw me to her front door. 'You'll want to reheat that. There's nothing worse than trying to eat it when it's cold, Jonathan tells me.' She had packaged up a piece of quiche and a large quantity of guilt, both sealed in a stifling amount of cling film.

'Thanks for your time,' I said from the safety of her doorstep, as though I were a salesperson concluding a pitch. 'We'll talk soon?'

'I'll be in touch. Take care now,' she hesitated before adding, 'Maggie.'

She'd always struggled to keep up with my names.

EIGHT

It took ten days and a lie to get the boys to visit the house. I hated being deceitful generally, but especially when it came to my children. But after calling them both, calling their homes, and even resorting to emails, only to be met with placeholder responses about how busy they were and how we should all catch up properly soon – that ambiguous and non-committal term we all use when agreeing to a future arrangement with heavy reluctance – I resorted to a text message drafted to sound panicked. I told them both that I thought a pipe had burst in the kitchen and I couldn't find an available plumber and there was water everywhere and I simply didn't know what to do and could they–

I was met with a near immediate response from Otis. He said that he and Finn would both come round when they'd finished work for the day. They didn't work together but their offices were nearby to each other, and I knew they occasionally car-shared when their meeting schedules allowed for it. Otis was an accountant while Finn worked as a freelance financial advisor to organisations in the charity sector. Their work-life experiences had been vastly different when they first stepped into their respective industries: one of them working with companies that dealt in millions of pounds on an annual basis; the other working with small collectives trying to gather enough money to make a substantial change in the world. To begin with they had both spoken to me often of the people and businesses they encountered in their work lives. Now, they hardly spoke to me – at all. For all of us work had become a haven, a buffer, something we could discuss one nominated speaker at a time whenever they happened to visit for dinner. I suspect that's why we stopped talking about work in between visits; it dried up the well of conversation for when we were in person. Though on this occasion, I thought the conversation I was throwing them into was more akin to an ocean – shark-infested waters – than it was a quiet village watering hole.

I'd gone to great lengths to clear the kitchen table free of my workload. The only thing remaining was a slim cardboard folder inside which were two lists. They differed to my usual ones though. Instead of detailing a string of jobs to complete or a week of groceries to buy, one list was pros and the other cons – for a decision that I had considered made, up until seeing my sister. I wasn't sure what Bernie's intention had been. But the comment about good – about finally doing some good, in all this – rang in my ears like tinnitus for days after seeing her. I would rest my head against a cold pillowcase at night and feel the bite of the comment; a shovel hitting grains of sand over and again: '...now's your chance.'

I had just laid the final place setting when the doorbell went. They hadn't agreed on a time, but I'd had the lentil cottage pie resting in the oven for nearly forty minutes already and I took a small joy in the serendipity of the moment. On my way past I knocked the heat down on the oven and then trod to the front door. It was clear that Otis and Finn had both gone home after work; their suits had been replaced by roughed up jeans and baggy T-shirts, as though they were both braced for physical graft. Otis smiled and gestured with what I thought must be his effort at a toolbox. His father's toolkit was in the garden shed, I remembered then, my having moved it from house to house with me; a quiet implication that I might eventually find use for any of the contents, though I couldn't remember a time when I had.

'The cavalry has arrived,' he said, and Finn laughed.

'Let's see the state of the pipework before we make any promises, mate.'

Finn was the youngest of the two. I never knew how much he remembered of Edward. He'd been so young still that I thought – or maybe I only hoped – he'd managed to block out much of what happened; small black holes that had opened in his living memory. Otis, on the other hand, remembered everything. I imagined he would be the harder sell out of the two of them; assuming I had anything to sell them at all. When I thought like that, I thought perhaps I'd made up my mind already to help my husband. But when I thought of it in those terms – *help* him – the pendulum swung again, and I realised I was yet to make a decision at all.

'Do I smell...' Otis turned his nose into the air. 'Did you cook?'

I managed a thin smile. 'I did. Lentil cottage pie.'

Finn narrowed his eyes. 'In a flooded kitchen?'

A beat of silence passed before Otis sighed. 'I see.'

'You'd better come in.' I stepped aside to make way for them. They both paused to kiss my cheek as they walked through the hallway. Following the scent, they trod along to the kitchen then while I closed and locked the door. I thought I heard a mumble of something pass between them. 'Can I get anyone anything to drink?'

Otis was inspecting the kitchen with his hands on his hips. 'Do you have lemonade?'

He always asked for lemonade, which is why I'd bought a bottle earlier in the day when I ventured out to repurchase the ingredients for the cottage pie. 'Of course. Finn?'

'I'll just have the same.' He was already pulling out a chair at the table. He chose a seat that gave him a view of the garden. 'If we'd known it wasn't a plumbing issue, we could have brought gardening gear instead. It looks a bit...'

'Wild,' Otis finished.

'It's on my list,' I answered as I set down two glasses of lemonade. 'You'll have something to eat?'

'Be rude not to now we're here,' Otis said as he took a seat next to his brother. I couldn't decide whether it was intended to be a cutting remark or a sincere one – or whether there was a possibility it might somehow be both. 'You could have just asked us if you wanted us to come over for dinner, Mum, you didn't have to–'

'She did,' Finn interrupted him in a quiet voice.

They were both silent while I dished out three servings of cottage pie. I had two Tupperware containers on the side, too, to serve up portions for them to take home to Emilia and Alice. For once, I was glad the girls hadn't come with them. I carried their portions first and then went to get my own before taking a seat opposite them both.

'Don't stand on ceremony,' I smiled, 'dig in, please.'

Finn started by peeling away the burnt crust of the mashed potato. It was his favourite part of any pie I made.

'How's work?' Otis asked after his first mouthful, and I felt my stomach twist.

In answer, I pushed forward the single folder that I'd left on the table.

Finn laughed. 'Did you bring work to dinner with you?'

'There are two lists in there.' I tapped the closed mouth of the cardboard. 'One of them is reasons for and the other is reasons against, but I wanted to speak to you–'

'For and against what?' Otis interrupted me as though I were a work colleague he had no patience for. His work had made him brittle around the edges. From experience, I knew it could often take him some time to reacclimatise to talking to people like they were normal people, rather than someone clogging up his inbox.

I tried to match the professionalism of his tone. 'Speaking to your father.'

Finn immediately began choking on what I thought was a mouthful of lentils, and I was reminded of Bernie. I wondered whether choking was somehow a stock response to this proposal. *Had I choked at all when Kitsell and Thompson were here?* I tried to remember but couldn't, and in those painful seconds of silence while Finn struggled to get his breath back, that detail suddenly became dreadfully important.

Otis sat opposite me narrow-eyed, waiting for more information.

'He's dying, Otis–'

'I know, I read the news.'

I tried to ignore the small lacerations I felt from his answer. 'He's dying, and he wants to talk about things that happened.' I shook my head and corrected myself. 'He wants to talk about things that he did.'

'Why you?' Finn asked. 'Why not the police?'

'I don't know, Finny.'

'Because the man's a fucking sadist, that's why.' Otis speared a carrot ring as though it had personally offended him. 'You can't possibly be thinking of agreeing to this.'

'She is or we wouldn't be here.'

'Mum?' Otis pushed me.

'I wasn't, no. And then I spoke to Bernie about it.' I fumbled with the cardboard folder to free the lists, as though anything written on either sheet of paper was likely to diffuse the situation now. 'She said– Bernie, she made a comment about doing something right, getting something right in all of this and... It could help a lot of people, to know.'

'Everyone already knows full well what he did,' Otis snapped.

'But they don't, do they?' Finn spoke in a small boy voice. He looked from his brother to me and back again, and when neither of us offered an answer he said, 'There are things that people never found out about, right?' He turned back to me. 'More girls, that's what they want to know about?'

'And the dead one they never found.' Otis made it sound unreasonable, for the police to want to know. I hated that so many people had forgotten Lucy's name. 'So the police want you to do their jobs for them, essentially?'

'It isn't the police's fault that your father has asked for this. It's your father's fault and–'

'Because he hasn't done enough damage to this family already?'

'Will you just let Mum finish a sentence?' Finn used his big boy voice then.

Otis shrugged and started to tuck into his dinner. It made this whole situation feel like a minor family dispute, rather than something that might fracture us down to our core.

'I don't know what to do,' I admitted plainly then, and Finn looked saddened. 'I don't know what to do because I have carried this, and I know you two have carried this. But the girls– The women's families have carried this, too. This might be a way for them to find what they're looking for, and for them to draw a line beneath it and...' I petered out when Otis looked up at me, and I saw a smirk that reminded me of his father. 'What?'

'You've made your fucking mind up, Mum.'

'Otis, don't speak to her like that. She's trying to explain.'

'There's nothing for her *to* explain. She's going to drag us back into the same media circus that we had as kids. Emilia and Alice are going to find out *exactly* why we never mention having a dad. We'll be dragged through the fucking papers *again–*'

'I'm going to make it a condition,' I interrupted him, '*if* I do it, it's a condition of my doing it that it stays confidential.' I reached across the table to them both; a hand held out to each. Otis spotted the gesture and shook his head, but Finn kindly reached back to me. I felt buoyed by his kindness against the tide of Otis's rage. 'I don't want to be involved in this, Otis, but I am, and I have been for a very long time. But I won't let you two be involved, I won't let you be brought into it all again.'

Otis's eyes were slits. He didn't need to say that he believed me or trusted me; I could see that neither feeling was there. 'Okay,' he answered, flatly. He had given in too easily. When the sea rose for high tide, it never slipped away with a single word on the matter. Otis had always been the same. With a painful squeal of chair against floor he pushed back from the table then with such a force that his lemonade spilled. 'Do you know what, I've suddenly lost my appetite for this. Finn, I'll speak to you later, mate, all right? Mum,' he stepped around the table and kissed the crown of my head but the heaviness of it made the action more aggressive than it was tender, 'always a pleasure.'

Finn flinched when the front door slammed. 'He just needs time.'

'I can understand that.'

We spent another thirty minutes pushing food around our plates before Finn left, too. I dropped my pros and cons lists into the kitchen bin, and scraped the remains of our dinners on top. It was shortly followed by the bulk load of remaining cottage pie. I hadn't needed the Tupperware after all.

NINE

Town was peppered with so many coffee shops now. I'd been sitting in one for twenty minutes before realising it was in fact not where Kitsell and I were meant to be meeting at all. He'd chosen somewhere a further five-minute walk down the road I was on. *So at least I got the right road,* I thought as I spotted him sitting in a window seat. He waved when he saw me, a smile fixed in place, and for a flicker of a moment it felt as though we were only old friends meeting for tea and time to talk. I'd called him the night before to ask if we could discuss things, face to face and preferably without Thompson. Otis had shown me enough hostility four days before and the last thing I needed was for another biased commentator to become embroiled in the decision-making process of whether I would or would not see Edward. Of course, though, Otis had been right when he said that I had by and large made the decision already...

I hadn't realised until five hours or so after they'd left, when I was staring into the hollow dark over my bed – having long abandoned sleep by then. But of course, he'd been right. There was a part of me – influenced by Bernie, perhaps, though I was under no delusions that this might do anything to repair our relationship – that had already decided I would agree to Edward's terms. Otherwise, what was the worth in having mentioned it to the boys at all? When Finn was younger – old enough to understand that his father was in prison but perhaps not quite old enough to understand the magnitude of why – he'd exchanged letters with Edward. They had only spoken a handful of times, that I knew of, before Finn had quietly told me during one bedtime tuck-in that he didn't want to speak to his father anymore. After that, I had returned all of Edward's letters to the prison authorities – and soon after that, I moved house with the boys anyway, and Edward couldn't have continued his efforts even if he'd desperately wanted to. Otis, as far as I knew, hadn't known and still didn't know any of this. He had cut his father out from the time of his arrest; a rotten tooth yanked from the root that left a space for Otis to tongue and bother throughout his angry teenage years, as though he took a sordid pleasure in reminding himself that he was fatherless. I wondered whether that accounted for their markedly different responses to the news of my talking to him – potentially talking to him – now.

'What can I get you?' Kitsell asked. There was an awkward moment where it looked as though he were about to hug me, and I wondered whether he, too, felt that aura of friends meeting for tea. 'I'm on green tea but I highly recommend against that.'

I laughed. 'Why are you drinking it?'

He waved the question away. 'Some bloody detox or another that my daughter has got me on.' I tried to recall whether he'd ever mentioned a daughter before now. *He must have done*, I thought, *but why don't I remember her?* 'Tea or coffee?'

I took a cursory glance at the menu behind the counter. It always overwhelmed me to see the many flavours and styles of coffee available now. It catapulted me far beyond the comfort zone of my instant granules that I used at home. I was never sure what the equivalent was, if such a thing existed in these watering holes.

'I'll have a breakfast tea,' I answered.

'Wise choice. Do you want anything to eat?'

'I'm fine, thank you.' Food still felt like an insurmountable task on the average day. I had got through three loaves and two blocks of mature cheddar, but anything more than grated cheese sandwiches made my stomach tidal.

'I'll just be a minute then. Get yourself settled.'

From the vantage point of the window it was easy enough to distract myself with the outside world. There was a woman across the street fighting with a pushchair that was carrying more than its recommended load-bearing weight in shopping. A man nearly walked into her, his tie flapping in the autumn wind and his phone fixed to his ear, and his urgency made it easy for me to imagine that he was rushing to a meeting – or from a meeting, perhaps, in a hurry now to get back to his desk. A group of young girls volleyed with the flurries of traffic, trying to choose their opportune moment to get from one side of the street to the other. On my side of the street, my vision of everyone else was temporarily hazed out by an older woman who was struggling to juggle a single tote bag of shopping while thumbing something into her phone. It wasn't until she was nearly out of my sightline that I realised she and I were likely the same age. And I wondered how many of them had heard of Edward O'Connor; how many of them must be glad of the news.

'There we are.' Kitsell set down a tray with a teapot, cup and saucer, a small milk bottle and a timer. 'Apparently breakfast tea is such a rarity in these places people need actual guidance on how long to let it brew for,' he narrated with good humour, gesturing to the squat blue egg timer in front of me. 'You're sure you don't want anything else?'

I smiled. 'You don't need to handle me with kid gloves, but thank you.'

'That wasn't my intention,' he held up his hands in defence, 'but a little kindness goes a long way, and I'd wager you need a bit of kindness. I can't imagine we've put you in an easy spot, with what Thompson and I asked of you the other day.'

'It isn't you that's asked it of me.'

He sighed. 'Well, no, I suppose that's right.'

'Have you seen him?' I asked then, and neither of us felt the need for a qualifier to explain which 'him' I was referring to.

Kitsell sipped his green tea and winced. 'I have.'

'And he refused to speak to you?'

'Not at all. He and I had a nice old chat about prison and life and, well, you. He mentioned the boys but I swerved that conversation.' I flashed him a look of gratitude that he clearly understood. 'It isn't my place to talk about your boys, and I know how I'd feel if it was my daughter in all this.'

'How would you feel?'

He looked out of the window as he answered. 'Like she'd been through enough.'

I wrapped my hands around the teapot and pressed my palms firmly against its body. The egg timer hadn't given me permission to pour my tea yet. 'They really have, both of them.'

'All of you,' Kitsell corrected me. He did something so unusual then, so entirely unexpected, that I flinched against it: he reached out and softly squeezed my shoulder. 'I know there was all the nonsense, Maggie, about... she must have known, how could she not have known, but... Thompson and I, we never had any doubts, none then, none now. We know that you've been through the ringer as much as anyone.'

'Not as much as the mothers whose children are dead,' I snapped.

He took another sip of his drink. 'Different people have different traumas.'

I nodded in soft agreement with him. The sand had run through on the timer and I immediately poured the tea out. I needed something to busy myself with.

'How many times would I have to see him?'

Kitsell hesitated before he said, 'I wish there was an easy answer to that.'

'As many times as it takes?'

'Essentially, yes.'

I nodded. 'We'd be in prison?'

'You would. We'd bring you in as a visitor. You wouldn't need a wire or anything as extreme as that, but we would give you a tape recorder to keep on the table with you, for anything that went under our radar. Even though we'd be watching the entire time, through the looking glass, and we should, in theory, be able to hear everything Edward says that way, too. The recorder would be a precaution.'

I splashed milk into my tea. 'How many people would know I was there?'

Kitsell's brow pulled together but then smoothed as he realised the meaning in my question. 'You're worried about the press?'

'Not for myself,' I rushed to add, 'I'm worried about the boys.'

'That, I can understand.'

'So I would need to know they were protected in all of this, too.'

'You want it to be confidential, what we're doing? Because I can tell you now, the police aren't in the habit of bowing to the demands of convicted serial killers. We're not exactly going to be shouting about this ourselves.'

'I need to know, for certain, that no one will be shouting about it.'

'Maggie, I– There's no way for me to promise you that.'

It was an answer I'd expected, of course. Kitsell wasn't a magician nor a miracle worker, and there was no way that any one person involved in this plan could guarantee that any one person mightn't open their mouth to the wrong person at the wrong time. And before I knew it there would be reporters outside the house again, camera crews at the boys' offices, another name change. I took a deep breath to try to steady the rising tide. If I looked in the face of it for too long, it would be enough, I knew, to turn me back towards the safety of shore – where Edward could remain someone else's problem.

'There are precautions we can talk through,' he added then, and I found that that made breathing easier. 'That'll be something to thrash out with the current investigating officers, who you'd need to meet before this went full ahead. You might have guessed that Thompson and I are both out of the force now, technically.' He paused to sip at his tea. 'We're both on this in a consultancy fashion, and there's a new team, very good people, very *kind* people,' he leaned heavily on that, 'who are happy to meet you and discuss things in more detail, and Thompson and I can be involved in those discussions, too, to make sure you've got fair representation all round.'

It was too much information all at once. I took two thirsty mouthfuls of tea and touched my fingers to my lips afterwards, feeling the burn of heat move through my mouth.

'Maggie?' Kitsell touched my shoulder again. 'You don't have to do this.'

I smiled in the face of his generosity. It was an affectionate thing for him to say. But–

'Of course I do,' I answered plainly, my voice sounding like someone else's.

59

TEN

It wasn't quite uncanny; not in the traditional, psychoanalytical sense of the term. Nevertheless, there was something both familiar and not about walking into the police station. The posters in the waiting room were different to those that had been displayed some twenty years ago, which is when I thought I last must have been here. There were eyes staring out from the walls, though I couldn't determine whether it was intended to note police watching us all, or criminals. There were greyscale pictures of people cowering in corners, overlayed with information about psychological abuse. There was a noticeboard of missing individuals that cleanly broke away a corner of my heart. I couldn't remember the exact or fine details of the posters from last time though. I could only remember they were watercolour every time I came in here; either from tears or panic, or both. Now, I thought of those visits as a kind of dream sequence, as though I'd spent a significant period of my life in an un-reality. I wondered whether, twenty years from now, whether I would look back on this moment and feel the same. Assuming I had another twenty years in me, that is; though I prayed to someone that if I were looking back, again, I wouldn't be looking back from inside another police station waiting area.

The seats were uniform blue and battered. Beyond that, there weren't many decorative features to distract myself with. The woman behind the main desk had told me to take a seat, but from the layer of grime coated on each, I wondered, worried, at what I might carry out of the building with me if I were to perch on one of them. So instead I paced the same four or five steps, one direction and then the other, staring hard at the walls and scanning black and white posters about drug abuse.

The automatic doors opened and the sound of men's chatter pulled me around to that direction. I'd never been so thankful to see Kitsell and Thompson in my life. They were both wearing smart but casual attire, and smiles that made me think they must be talking about literally anything but what they were here for. Both men looked far too relaxed, far too involved in easy conversation, to have been discussing their plan of attack for extracting vital evidentiary materials from the mind of a warped—

'Maggie, have you been waiting long?' Kitsell gave my elbow a squeeze with the same familiarity he'd shown at the coffee shop. I shook my head in a lie and he smiled as though he could tell. 'Let's get you in, shall we? I'll just go and have a word with— Lisa, any chance...' He trailed off as he wandered over to the desk sergeant.

'You're doing the right thing, you know?' Thompson said then. He was standing closer to me than I'd realised, speaking in a lowered voice as though to shut the world out of the exchange. I turned to face him but saw that he was staring in Kitsell's direction still. It felt like covert communication. 'It's bollocks that you're having to do it at all, mind you. But you are doing the right thing, for the families if not for yourself. Though they talk a lot about closure now, don't they? Maybe this is your chance for that.'

I had made it this far through the debacle of my life without the need or want of closure so my remaining years certainly would have been fine without it, too. It felt rude to point that out, though, particularly when I thought this was likely Thompson's version of being comforting. He wasn't quite as adept at it as Kitsell was.

'Right, I've got the keys to the castle,' Kitsell closed the distance between us all, 'or rather, the passcode to the office space. Strange being here as a guest, isn't it?' He directed the question to Thompson more so than me. I imagined they could both guess how I felt about being a guest here again. 'I'll lead the way.'

Kitsell headed towards one of the side doors leading off from the waiting room. Thompson gestured for me to follow ahead, and then he stepped in behind me. This is how they'd escorted me through last time, and the procedure of entering the belly of the building flanked by two senior detectives felt like a muscle memory I wasn't aware I had stored until now. I wondered what else of this would become familiar over the course of the morning: would I remember the offices once I saw them again? Would there be the same corkboard of evidence, ineffectively covered with a too small piece of fabric when I entered the space? Would they all stop and stare, as so many of them had done last time?

It was inevitable that there would be new faces involved in today's events. The true purpose of the meeting was to introduce me to the new senior investigators, in fact. But I wondered how many of the old team members might be there, too – or, more pertinently, whether they would still suspect me of having known all about it, or whether that judgement would have withered at all in the intervening years. *A woman can only hope*, I thought with a breath that stretched itself all the way down my abdomen.

Kitsell led us through another two doorways, nodding and saying hello to people as we went. It was clear that, retired from the force or not, he and Thompson were still regulars in the building. It wasn't only that everyone seemed to know them, but rather, everyone seemed to want contact with them. The greetings were so enthusiastic in some cases that it wouldn't have surprised me had some of the younger detectives held out a hand to touch or high-five their experienced forebears. I was almost disappointed when it didn't happen; that, at least, would have cut through some of the tension that hovered around me, a cartoon smog that I struggled to breathe through, especially as I walked further into the building.

After what felt like minutes, Kitsell eventually pushed through into a room that resembled a boardroom rather than a busy office space. It was almost anticlimactic. There were two people sitting at a table that looked designed for at least twelve. They had been talking, but their chatter faded when they realised someone had entered the room. Kitsell and Thompson said their familiar hellos to the new people and I realised in those seconds that these must, in fact, be the new detectives. An older woman with a curt bob, fighting to allow for natural curls and waves that, if I could guess, I would say she must have tried to tame or straighten that morning. She was friendly with Kitsell and Thompson, but I took note of the fact that she didn't even look at me after saying hello to them. Instead, she started to shuffle away the paperwork that had been splayed in front of her, herding half of the documents into a cardboard folder and leaving the others in a neat stack on the table. Meanwhile, her younger, boyish colleague – his hair in what I can only think to describe as a designer quiff complete with a fade that would have rendered the teenage versions of my boys envious – said hello first to Kitsell and Thompson and then, I was relieved to see, to me.

'You must be Maggie?' He held out a hand in greeting. It wasn't until I accepted that I realised I was shaking. 'I'm DS Newell.' I corrected my thinking then. *He can't be* that *young*. 'This is my colleague DI Rule.'

As though prompted, the woman stood and crossed the room to me then. At least now she was smiling. 'I can't tell you how much we appreciate you offering to come in and help us,' she said with a handshake so firm that I wanted to cradle my limb in comfort when it was returned to me. 'You can probably imagine how tense things have been, since Edward implied that there were other cases he wanted to discuss. It's the bite many of us have waited years for.' As though remembering Kitsell and Thompson were present just then, she gestured to them. 'Though I imagine that's something you likely know.'

'He's implied there are more?' I asked, looking from her to Kitsell and Thompson.

Kitsell nodded. 'We've always known, Maggie,' he answered in a tone that was somewhere between gentle and patronising. I expected him to tilt his head and add 'Haven't we?' to the end of his sentence. 'But yes, he's been very transparent about other cases existing. He's just less transparent about what the other cases *are*, which is...'

'Difficult,' Rule finished.

'The bloke really is a tosser,' Thompson added in a voice that was in no way quiet enough for any of us not to hear the remark. 'Sorry, did I say that out loud?' he added, but only after Kitsell had nudged him in the side.

'Maggie, do you want to take a seat?' Newell was sitting already by then, and he gestured to the chair opposite him. Rule returned to her seat, by his side, and I took careful note of where Kitsell and Thompson positioned themselves. A deep wash of relief moved over me when I saw them move to my side of the table.

'Obviously, our old friends here have filled you in on some of the details,' Rule smiled at Kitsell and Thompson again then, 'but I'm keen to know what your understanding of the situation is as it stands.'

There was a long pause before I realised that she wasn't going to give me any further guidance on what I was expected to say. 'Edward is dying and he has things he wants to confess to, and he's said I'm the only person he'll speak to.'

'Stage four cancer,' Newell said, looking through some of the sheets still in front of him. 'He's refusing treatment,' he looked up and flashed me a tight smile, 'said something about it being his time.'

I narrowed my eyes. That didn't sound like Edward. Though of course, I hardly knew the man anymore. Something caught at the back of my throat, accompanied by a horrid, nagging thought: *I didn't know him to begin with.*

'And you're prepared to visit the prison?' Rule clarified.

I nodded. 'Will it be once?'

She glanced quickly at Kitsell before she answered. 'It's unlikely.'

'Edward likes to dance around the topic of conversation.' Thompson smiled at me when I looked across at him. 'I'd wager that, given how long it's been since you've spoken, it's going to take a bit of time to get through to what we actually want to know.'

'Which is a good lead in...' Rule freed a piece of paper from her file and slid it across the table. 'We've drafted some talking points, things to try to steer him towards. Inevitably, he will try to steer you away from them. It's a rouse and a rascal's trick, especially given that we're bowing to his demands here. I think, Maggie, our proposal is that if we don't get anything by the end of the second visit then we reconsider putting you through this at all. How does that sound to you?'

It sounded like someone had taken the covering off a beehive. Her words rushed around me in a swarm while I tried to read through the list of questions in front of me. There were many there about Lucy – Where is she? Why wasn't she left with the others? – but there were other names I didn't recognise, places and times and accusations and–

'Maggie?' Kitsell touched my shoulder as he spoke. 'Are you okay?'

'I...' I looked from one to the other, met their questioning glances with an audible turn in my stomach. 'I...' My mouth was desert dry; it reminded me of being hungover. Drunk with Edward. At university. Still young enough to afford mistakes. 'I don't know,' I managed to answer. As I looked through the list of accusations I found myself thinking, *I don't know that I can ever be okay again.* But that same familiar beast of guilt clambered onto its haunches to plague me with another wail of a question:

After what he did, why do you think you have the right to be?

ELEVEN

I'd never been inside a prison before. And as another door clanged closed behind me, I thought that I likely hadn't missed out on anything by not visiting sooner. There were two detectives ahead of me, two former detectives behind. Rule and Newell were weighted down by notebooks and folders, as though they were preparing for a study session in the adjoining room. Kitsell was only weighed down by platitudes that he occasionally muttered, every time he saw me flinch at a sound in the jailhouse. Thompson didn't appear weighed down by anything physical nor emotional, but I'd sensed a tension in the bunch of his shoulders when he'd collected me from the house that morning.

'We'll just settle in here for a second, Maggie.' Newell held a door open for me. I'd noticed how he insisted on using my name like a comma, though I couldn't work out whether it was to ground me or to try to demonstrate that he saw me as a person rather than a snitch – or perhaps, someone enabling snitching.

Rule had walked in ahead already and she had split her bag open on the table. The first thing she removed was a tape recorder; *my* tape recorder, I assumed. Then she pulled out a full pad, a sheet of paper with both print and annotations on, a bottle of water. It was a veritable Mary Poppins's bag of police work.

'Feel free to take a seat,' she said without looking at anyone in particular.

I didn't though. Instead, I was drawn to the window that looked in on another room beyond it. That would be my cell for the morning, I thought. A metal table with two chairs opposing each other. There were two closed doors leading into the room, too. One for me and one, I assumed, for my husband to come strolling in. *Will he stroll, or will he be forced to shuffle with cuffed ankles?*

'Will he be wearing handcuffs?' I asked without turning. Kitsell answered.

'The whole time.'

'We're not taking any chances with anything like that, Maggie,' Rule reassured me. She moved through the room then, coming to a stop at my side. She handed me a bottle of water, which I accepted with a mumbled thank you. 'We've agreed to an hour, no more and no less. The guards are aware of that, too, and you can bet a dollar that they'll be timing Edward from the other side of that door.'

I sucked in a greedy inhale and felt a judder in my chest. 'I imagine this is a strange situation for everyone involved.'

'Mm.' Rule set a hand on my back, her palm flat between my shoulder blades. 'It is, but it's also the right thing to be doing.'

'It's okay,' I turned to face her, 'Kitsell has told me times a-plenty that it's the right thing. I don't intend to back away from it now. Not at the first hurdle, anyway.' I hadn't ruled out backing away from the second hurdle though. The thought of seeing Edward sent tidal waves through my stomach and I was *deeply* concerned that the black coffee I'd managed for breakfast would come rushing back as soon as I saw him in person. But still I flashed the detective a thin smile, before I walked to the central table where the other three were gathered and talking among themselves.

'Super easy to operate.' Newell picked up the recorder and spoke as though we'd been in mid-conversation. 'Click here to start, you don't even need to worry about pressing anything else after that. We'll turn it off when we collect you from the room. There's a tape in here, obviously, but there's also a tape in there,' he gestured to the adjoining room behind us, 'so we'll have additional footage of everything.'

'And we'll be listening the whole time,' Thompson added.

'Is there anything you want to ask, or discuss before it starts?' Rule asked.

'No, thank you, I–'

My sentence broke off when a door opened somewhere behind us. I didn't turn, only held my breath and waited for a further noise. And then it came, a jovial tone of voice, a laugh I remembered too well, and in that moment I felt a surge of hate for the way in which he had seemingly bonded with the guard who was chattering back to him. I couldn't discern what they were saying in among the sea of sound batting against my eardrums. But I could hear the ease of it. It felt as though someone had held a conch shell either side of my head, the ocean rushing about in the spaces between them, while someone held a conversation on the shore somewhere. *This is what it feels like to drown*, I thought and no sooner had that occurred to me and I was gasping for air. Rule said something but I couldn't hear her. As though in answer, I could only turn and search the room in front of me now.

His hair had greyed but somehow it suited him. It was cut closely against his head though there were the beginnings of curls at the base, encroaching onto his neck, in the same way his hair had always done when he was due for an appointment with his barber. He was wearing a jumpsuit, pale blue in colour, though it was a faded blue, a too many washes blue, rather than something that had been deliberately tinged to reflect a baby boy shade. Kitsell had been right; his hands were cuffed, and he'd placed them on the centre of the table to make a display of them. I watched as the guard leaned down to add an additional cuff to one ankle, fixing Edward against the table that was bolted to the floor. I saw him in montage then, Edward through the years, though there was a blank space where his forties and fifties should have been. He was still an attractive man, even now, when time was so clearly against him. He flashed that wide shark smile at the guard and thanked him, before being left alone in the room. The longer I stared, the more it felt as though Edward was a perverse art installation, put on display to make someone – *me* – feel things. *There you are*, I thought with another judder of a breath, *my husband the serial murderer*.

'How are the boys?'

'I'm not here to talk about the boys.'

He huffed, a near-laugh. 'You're going to have to talk to me about something.'

'This isn't a social call, Edward.' His name tasted like burnt toast in my mouth; there was a lingering unpleasantness after I'd said it. I had managed to go so long without saying his name at all, and there was a growing resentment then at just how often I had said it in the past four weeks. 'You said you wanted to talk to me.'

'Confess.'

My head snapped up. I had tried to avoid looking directly at him, as though he harboured the ability to turn my shaking body to stone – or something that might disintegrate much easier than that.

'I said I wanted to confess to you.' He shuffled forward in his seat to lessen the gap between us and I fought the urge to lean backwards. 'You used to be the first person I told *everything* to, remember that? I'd call you with good news, or come strolling in with a nice conversation I'd had at work, or even–'

'Come rolling home in the dead of night and tell me about a woman you'd murdered.'

He looked surprised by the comment. In fact, I had surprised myself to a degree, too. I had thought it a flicker of a moment before saying it. But I was amazed my voice had held long enough for the words to knock into a sentence.

'Well, no,' he leaned back then, as though I'd ruined the moment, 'I never told you that. I'll bet people thought you knew, though, didn't they?' He seemed pleased by that thought. *Bastard.* 'Credit to people, it's unlikely that a wife mightn't know what her husband was up to for *all* of those years. Are you sure?'

I narrowed my eyes and felt my head twitch; a bird inspecting something buried in the ground still, shifting the soil.

'Are you *sure* you didn't know?'

'You know bloody well I didn't know,' I snapped back – and that pleased him, too. I knew he was trying to stir a rise in me and I was determined not to, *gritting* my teeth not to, but you cannot be married to someone for fifteen years without learning the sensitive parts of them; the bits that hurt when pressed against, the bits that ache. 'You're wasting time and from what I hear you don't have much, so if you have something to say you'd better.'

'Six months, they reckon.'

I hadn't been referring to the cancer. There was only twenty-one minutes of our hour left. We had already danced around the boys, my life and their lives, and plenty more besides that I refused to discuss or divulge. And now, the cancer – which is exactly what he was, I thought then, a rotting, growing tumour of–

'Does it bother you, my dying?'

–something that needed to be cut out.

'No.'

His head snapped back as though I'd slapped him. 'Are you trying to hurt me, Lind?'

'It's Maggie, now, and–'

'And that's what I call you, is it, Maggie?'

I ignored the interruption and tried to hold my tone steady. 'You don't matter enough for me to try and hurt you, Edward.' I opened my water bottle and took a slow sip, to give the comment time to breathe and swell in the room. Then I capped the bottle and clenched my lower belly. 'Tell me about the girls.'

'Which girls?'

'Tell me about Lucy.'

A strange noise crept out of him; one that seemed to denote hesitation. 'I'm not sure I'm ready to talk about Lucy yet.'

'Then what are you ready to talk about?'

He smiled, that same shark smile, and I wondered how it would feel to actually slap the man. Would Rule storm in and wrestle me out of the room? Would they do nothing at all, and let me have a free hit – more than *one* free hit? I narrowed my eyes and wondered, and Edward only laughed.

'Do you remember that family holiday we had in Brighton?'

'Edward...'

'That's it, that's the tone you used!' He pointed and shifted in his seat with too much enthusiasm. 'When Otis came back up the beach and he was *soaked* to his core with mud, because it was the worst time of year to try to get to the sea, but our boy, undeterred, he'd tried all the same. You must remember, *Mags*.

Think.' He awkwardly folded his hands as best as the cuffs would allow and leaned in towards me again. I swallowed hard and the sound of it dropped into my stomach. '*Think*, Maggie. What do you remember from that holiday?'

There was a horrid, sweating silence then. The walls shifted inwards, the bolts of the doors creaked, and my breath got caught somewhere between mouth and lungs. Edward looked at me searchingly and I wondered whether he was waiting for a happy memory to come tumbling out – the sad reality being that there were none left from those times. Edward from the boys' childhood was tainted by off-colour half-memories of what my husband must have been doing years later, when he was late home from work or going for his evening runs, returning muddied and exhausted and desperate for a shower. The Brighton holiday, *all* of the holidays, of which there had been many in the earliest days of our parenthood, it was only greyscale now; a faded Polaroid.

'Think, Maggie.'

A door howled open from somewhere behind me and my head snapped around.

'DI Rule, always a pleasure,' Edward said.

'O'Connor,' she answered, her tone flat and her face neutral. 'Maggie, it's time.'

'But we hardly even got to the good part,' Edward answered for me. Meanwhile, I was already out of my seat and limping towards the door, my body that of a wounded animal now. 'Maggie,' he called my attention back and smiled, the folds of his face tucking awkwardly around the expression, 'I'll be seeing you...'

The water was uncomfortably cold now. It had started scalding hot and my skin had bloomed pink, one strip at a time as I slowly lowered myself into the water, my breath held against the heat. I usually preferred showers. I had showered twice when I got home from seeing Edward, two days ago now, convinced that I could rinse him off me. When the shower hadn't worked I'd resorted to baths; hot enough to make the pipes of the house moan. I must have been there for longer than I realised, my knees tucked against my chest and my arms wrapped around them, with nothing but the radio as background static. I had brought it up from the kitchen for company, though I wouldn't have been able to attest to a word anyone had said, on whatever programme happened to be on.

I moved around in my own swill. There were no bubbles; this wasn't intended to be that sort of bath. I could only hope that it would be hot enough to strip away the cells that had sat opposite the man, leaving me fresh – cleansed. I cupped cold water over my hair before deciding it would be more efficient to risk moving. I lay down, my breath catching this time against the cooler temperature rather than the heat, and soaked my hair through. That's when I half-heard the doorbell. It was a Saturday afternoon, and unlikely to be anything more important than a book delivery from my newest client. I had been contracted to write a string of academic lectures for a cluster of colleges up north; they were sending me textbooks to assist with the design. I held my breath and imagined the disgruntled postman outside, filling out a slip, juggling a substantial box. Though he mightn't bother, I thought then, he might only dump the box on the ground in the hopes that I would find it. I'd need to check outside when I emerged from my makeshift absolution.

With a deep breath I threw myself upright and that's when I heard the bell again.

'For goodness' sake.' I climbed out of the bath and wrapped myself inside a cotton ball of a dressing gown; even the soft of it felt rough against my skin, parts of which were still light pink. I grabbed a towel to rub at my hair. Water droplets flung out from it as I worked the towel against it, leaving a breadcrumb trail of my journey from upstairs bathroom to front door. Through the frosted pane I could see someone standing there, and I immediately had visions of flashing bulbs, the clicks of cameras, questions pressed against me. I tried to steady myself with a deep breath as I reached for the door handle. *It's been two days,* I reminded myself, *and Kitsell gave you his word that so few people knew what was happening...*

I yanked the door open with a force to find–

'Finn.'

He smiled his boyish smile and held up a paper bag that brandished the McDonald's logo. 'You forget to eat when you're stressed.'

'You eat takeaway when you're fretful.' I sidestepped to let him into the house. 'Come on, you probably need to heat that through by now.' Our nearest McDonald's was a ten-minute drive away which mightn't seem like much. However, our nearest McDonald's also boasted a less than desirable reputation for serving lukewarm meals at best. The smell of the food catapulted me back to when Finn and Otis were boys. Now, Finn was in the kitchen fiddling with twists on the oven to call up a low heat.

'I got you Coke Zero,' he turned to me with a half a litre drink in hand, 'is that okay?'

'Perfect, thank you.' It was also about all I could stomach. I had, at least, graduated from cheese sandwiches to tuna sandwiches; largely because I had run out of cheese a day ago, and I couldn't bring myself to go anywhere near a shop – anywhere near a newspaper stand I meant, of course – at the risk of seeing Edward's face or name glaring back at me.

After only one visit, I was already nursing a *deep* family of concerns that there would soon be a headline that mentioned The Wife – or worse still, mentioned me by name. Worse still again, anything that mentioned the boys. I had texted them both after my first meeting with their father, to let them know that it had happened, I was safe, and he'd asked about them. Otis hadn't extended me the courtesy of a reply; meanwhile, Finn had only reacted to the message with a thumbs-up emoji. To have him land on the doorstep now then, brandishing lukewarm comfort, was a truly welcome surprise.

'I'll just put everything in for a minute or two,' he said as he slid an oven tray of burger boxes and fries onto the top shelf. 'You can choose between a fish burger and a beef burger.'

I don't know what expression I wore, but apparently I'd made a face.

Finn laughed. 'You have to eat.'

'I am eating.'

He crossed the room to open the bin then, like I might have

done when he was a boy and I was trying to prove a point that an empty packet of Haribo did not constitute having had dinner. Finn lifted the lid to peer inside; his lips moved in small shifts, but he was muted.

'Two empty milk bottles, what looks like two empty bread sleeves, and approximately,' he bopped his head as he counted again, 'three tins of tuna?' He dropped the bin lid and walked to the table, pulling out a chair opposite to the one I'd let myself fall into. 'I'd wager there's an empty cheese bag under there somewhere, if I were willing to dig deep enough.' Finn reached across the table to grab my hand. He squeezed once, twice, to get my attention. 'Mum, I say this with so much love...' There was a spasm somewhere deep in my stomach. 'But you *have* to start sorting your recycling out.'

A laugh came tumbling out of me and in that moment I was so utterly overjoyed at the normalcy of it all, that I think I forgot why he was there.

'Shall I buy you another bin?'

'I have another bin, it lives outside. I usually throw things out there when I've finished.'

'But not this week?' He cocked an eyebrow at me and tutted. 'Shameful, Mum, honestly, think of the planet.' Finn stood and crossed back to the oven. He used a floral mitt to pull the tray of food free and distributed everything out between two plates. 'Fish or beef?'

'Fish.'

'Condiments?'

I smiled again then. Finn had come such a long way from being the small boy who shouted 'Ketchup' at the top of his voice whenever someone set a plate of food in front of him. Now, I told him there was ketchup and mayonnaise in the fridge and he ferreted out both before sitting at the table again.

'Can we talk about Dad?'

I had a fry halfway to my mouth but found that I needed to set it back down on the plate, as though the sudden weight of its thin frame was too much for me. I took a sip of my drink before I answered. 'Of course.'

'You said he asked about us?'

I nodded. 'I didn't tell him anything. It didn't feel right to.'

'I understand.' Finn broke off a chunk of his burger and tucked it into his mouth. 'Did he just ask how we were or…'

'How you were, what you were both doing with yourselves, whether you were well.'

'And you didn't tell him anything?'

I let a pause swell between us while I tried to decide whether I had courage enough to ask what I was thinking. 'Do you want me to tell him about you?'

Finn shook his head immediately and with conviction. 'No, thank you. He doesn't need to know anything about me, and Otis definitely wouldn't want him knowing about his life either.'

'Of course, I can understand that for you both.' I broke away a piece of burger bun and mouse-nibbled at it, to show willing. 'Have you heard from Ot–'

'Did he talk to you about Lucy?' The question, though reasonable, blindsided me still. 'Sorry, I– That's the main reason for you being there, isn't it? To help her family?'

I wasn't ready to tell Finn about the possibility of other women – or perhaps that should be, the certainty of other women. Instead, I nodded and sipped my drink again to buy myself a second to think, to breathe. 'He said he wasn't ready to talk about Lucy.'

Finn's brow wrinkled. 'Then what–'

'Brighton. He wanted to talk about Brighton.'

He laughed. 'Twenty years in prison and he wants to talk about family holidays.'

'Apparently so.'

'What about Brighton?'

'He told me to think hard about it.' I ripped another piece of bread free and placed it on my tongue. Chewing felt uncomfortable so I swallowed it whole. 'Think hard about it.'

Finn looked to be following the instruction with a greater conviction than I had managed. I had tried and tried to busy myself out of thinking about Brighton; beautiful Brighton with its tinged sea and its soft winds and its trademark two-penny pushers that appeared in great rows, inside every arcade. When the boys were young we had taken them to so many seaside towns, as though we had implicitly agreed to show them as much of the British coastline as we were able to. Going abroad had never interested us especially, apart from one disastrous trip to France when Otis developed a sickness on our journey there. Resultantly I had spent much of the holiday mopping his brow while Edward had entertained Finn.

'Is Brighton where he took that tumble?'

I shook my head. 'I don't...'

'Remember, he went for a run and he was *ages* and when he came back he said he'd fell, and this family had found him and— Am I making this up? Did this not actually happen?' He laughed.

The harder I thought the easier the memory became: Edward with grazed knees and the beginnings of a black eye, owed, he said, to the way in which his nose crushed up against the pavement when he fell. I tucked another piece of bread into my mouth and swallowed. The memory, suddenly tinged with a smog glow of suspicion, came back slowly in a clearer montage: Edward couldn't point out where he'd fallen, could hardly remember the family that had allegedly helped him home, but without stopping to actually help him into the holiday house.

He was bruised all over by the time we left for home two days later; blooms of purple and blue and black and– Finn was right, there had been a fall. *Had there been more than one?* But it hadn't been Brighton.

Brighton must be something else.

THIRTEEN

The thought of making food, whether I had to eat it or not, turned my stomach in riptides. It was the first time I was going to the food bank empty-handed though, and I didn't much like the thought of that either. On the walk there I entertained the idea of stopping at the local fish and chip shop and buying them out of everything warm. But I also appreciated that that was likely not what Claire had in mind when she asked that volunteers bring home-cooked meals for the visitors. I tried to find a happy medium by popping into Tesco and buying five Victoria sponges and five family-sized boxes of chocolate eclairs. While I was queueing for the checkout I decided that it didn't look like much insofar as penance for my sins though, and I rushed back to buy three boxes of apple turnovers and one of raspberry turnovers. I had cleared out their chilled cake selection.

'Having a party?' the woman said as she scanned through the items.

'It's for the local food bank.'

'Oh, that place on Camp Street?'

'Mm,' I mumbled in agreement while I ferreted through my bag for my purse.

'I see that place a lot and do you know, I always think, I should volunteer there.'

It seemed to be something that people always thought about, but very few people often did. I'd texted Rebecca earlier in the day to ask whether she was free to join me that evening, to which she replied, *Sorry – Zumba xx next time xx*. I didn't trust whether she actually had Zumba, or whether it was only a pointed comment towards the bargain we had struck when she last came over. But it had raised a smile in me at least, the first I'd managed for some days.

'Mind you, I spend so much time working, the last thing I want to do on a day off–'

'Is volunteer to help people less fortunate than you.' I flashed her a tight smile and handed over my card. 'Could I get a bag as well, please?'

'Of course.' Her tone was notably flatter than it had been to begin with and I thought I'd likely touched a nerve. 'Bag for Life okay?'

'Thank you.'

The woman packaged up the groceries and handed them over without comment.

'Thank you again,' I said as though gratitude might help to assuage some of her hurt feelings – or rather, assuage some of my guilt for having hurt her feelings. I would have accepted either outcome. Though from her expression it hadn't been a successful effort on my part.

It was a new weight of guilt that I carried from the shop with me then. Edward had always been the one who was rude to servers, sharp with people behind a till who asked whether we might donate to charity, downright unpleasant to anyone who stopped us in the street to ask the same. It was something I had always disliked about him, but never said. It hardly seemed worth mentioning to him now. In the grand scheme of things, I would have settled for Edward being obnoxious to strangers if it had meant his other misdemeanours were eradicated.

Since that first visit I'd noticed I was thinking of him more often than I had for years. It was an unwanted but, I thought, likely an unavoidable side effect of sitting down for a conversation with him again; which made the whole thing sound that bit more normal than it had been. Kitsell had called to see whether I was okay in the aftermath of it all. I'd lied, of course, and told him I was fine. The truth of that moment was that I'd been sitting on the living-room floor surrounded by photographs of family holidays when he called, trying to pull out the Brighton snaps as though they might reveal something of Edward's motivations in having mentioned the trip. I didn't tell Kitsell that. Nor did I tell Rule when she made an appearance on the phone call either, echoing Kitsell's question of whether I was *really* okay or not. Though I suspected her reasons had been more geared towards ensuring I was willing to go through with seeing Edward a second time, rather than truly wanting to check I was okay after the first occasion with him. That could have been scepticism on my part, but I would have set a strong wager that I was right.

'Maggie.' Claire caught my attention as soon as I was through the door. Her smile was warm, her demeanour welcoming; I could see how she'd found herself in this part of the volunteer sector. 'Did you buy out Tesco?' she joked.

I handed the bag over. 'I didn't have time to cook.'

'Oh, Maggie, you're not obliged to– Wow, hello!' She peered into the bag and started to shift items around to get a better view of the hidden ones. 'I'm half-tempted to put this in the volunteer room for the end of the shift.'

While I knew she was joking, I was bothered by a flicker of

worry then that I should have thought of the other volunteers. 'I...'

'Maggie,' she reached forward and rubbed softly at my upper arm, 'I'm only kidding around.' She looked at me with a softened expression then, as though searching my face for something. 'Is everything okay?'

I forced a smile. 'It's been a long day at work, that's all.' It was a lie. I was desperately behind with work, although not through lack of trying. I found my concentration withered like dehydrated fruit after an hour, and I was forced to take more regular breaks than I'd ever needed before. It was something else I was attributing to Edward. Though it frustrated me to afford him another influence in my life. 'Anyway, where do you want me this evening?'

Claire turned and pointed. 'We have a cold station in the far corner. Is that okay?'

'Anywhere is okay,' I smiled, 'do you want me to...' I gestured to the bag of cakes.

'I'll take these over to the tea and coffee station with me. Thank you so much, Maggie. Nothing better than a slice of cake with your cuppa, is there?' She winked and disappeared and my stomach growled after her.

The cold station was ill-favoured in comparison to the warmer spots around the room. Still, I served sandwiches cut neatly into triangles, bursting with tuna and onion, cheese and tomato, corned beef, and ham cuts. I wondered who had brought in so many uniform pieces. In between serving people, I busied myself by imagining someone at home making perfect measurements of the bread before slicing a knife through it; losing their temper, perhaps, when the filling began to ooze out against the pressure of the cut. It must have been a frustrating job, I decided, and a time-consuming one. The latter convinced me that it would be worth trying to make sandwich trays ahead of my next visit here. *The devil and idle hands*, I thought with a sharp intake of breath.

A woman arrived at the station then, with two young boys trailing behind her. She smiled but it was an expression loaded with shame; it pained me in the well of my stomach that she seemed not to want to meet my eye as she spoke.

'Can we have some of the tuna, and some of the ham, please?'

'Mum, have they got chicken slices?'

'No, baby, you can have ham.' She rubbed at the crown of the boy's head and then leaned forward to kiss him in the same spot. 'Ham will be just as good.'

He nodded with such resignment that it crossed my mind to walk out from behind the counter and hug the poor child to me. That, or rush back to Tesco for a loaf of bread and a packet of chicken slices.

I served out generous portions and spoke to the children directly. 'Ham for the young man.' His resignment looked more like relief when he took the paper plate from me. 'Tuna for the young gentleman?' The second child was older. He took the plate with thanks but seemed confused by my politeness towards him, which I thought was telling. Both children looked well turned out, with neat and clean clothes, and what looked to be freshly washed hair. The mother looked exhausted though, and I remembered that imbalance all too well.

'What will you have?' I asked her.

She smiled and rebuffed the offer. 'I'm fine, thank you.'

'Have you eaten from another station?'

The woman managed a weak laugh. 'They have, but I haven't. I'll wait until the end,' she lowered her voice to add, 'I don't want to take from someone who might need it more than me, you know?'

I nodded. 'I know.' Still, I pulled a paper plate from under the counter and started to add one of each sandwich to it. 'But just because someone else needs it doesn't mean you also don't.' I handed the plate across to her with a smile. 'Please?'

The younger boy tugged at the fringes of his mother's coat. 'Mum, take it.'

She acquiesced then. 'Thank you, I...' The woman shook her head lightly and let the end of the sentence die out. 'Thank you.'

'It's a pleasure.'

The three of them trod to a nearby table. The boys began tucking into their sandwiches as though it was the first thing they'd eaten that day, and I wondered which of the other stations they'd collected food from already. *I hope whoever it was was generous with them*, I thought as I watched the youngest pile his crusts at the edge of his plate, just like Finn would have done at that age. The mother said something to him before nodding and taking the crusts away; she set them on her own plate and picked at them with mouse mouthfuls.

I was over-anxious at the thought of their leaving without me having the chance to talk to them again. The station next to mine had fallen into a lull, owing to the pasta portions having nearly been cleared out; some of the containers looked scraped dry. So I leaned across to the volunteer for the station – a woman I didn't know; the volunteers were so often changing – and asked whether she wouldn't mind watching out for the sandwiches.

'Of course, of course,' she insisted. She came to straddle the space between the two food stations. 'Nature calls and all that.'

I smiled to feign my agreement and then reached for my handbag. By the time I crossed over to the family the boys had nearly finished their sandwiches; the eldest looked poised to help the mother with hers.

'I'm having a quick break. Do you mind?' I gestured to the

free seat at their table and the woman encouraged me to settle there. 'How were those sandwiches?' I asked the boys.

The youngest rubbed his stomach and plastered a dramatic smile across his full cheeks. 'Delicious. Even if it was ham and not turkey.'

I laughed along, and said nothing of the fact it had been chicken he longed for.

'They were nice, thank you.' The eldest was reserved, but still he managed a smile.

'I'm getting through mine,' the woman said around a mouthful, as though pre-empting or presuming she would be next in line. 'I really appreciate you having put a plate of them together for me. I didn't realise– Well, I didn't realise how much I needed something.'

'It's not a trouble, honestly. There are more...' I pointed to the food stand.

'No, really,' she pushed back, 'we've had enough. The boys are more than fed. And,' again she lowered her voice in the same way she had earlier, confiding a secret, excluding her young, 'this is honestly just to tide us over until payday. Their dad, he isn't–'

'Much use,' the eldest of the boys interrupted, having caught his mother's whisper.

She rolled her eyes. 'He isn't paying support at the moment, that's all.'

Her 'that's all' made a significant problem sound inconsequential, and I wondered how often the aforementioned father must withhold funds like this. It made me more determined, more desperate, even, to do something more than plate up sandwiches. I reached into my bag and pulled my purse free.

'Please don't think I'm overstepping,' I said as I searched the notes compartment. Everyone was so reliant on cards these days that I found I often kept a stash of small notes that I had no memory of putting there; it had been so long, in fact, that the first ten-pound note I withdrew didn't even look like legal tender. After searching, I placed two twenty-pound notes on the table and slid them across to her. 'I'd very much like to help.'

The woman's face turned and I thought *yes, yes I have overstepped.* With narrowed eyes she looked first at the money and then me again. 'Why?'

'Why would I like to help?'

She nodded. 'That's... Yeah, I mean, why?'

Penance, I thought with a flat smile. But I answered, 'Because I'm in a position to.'

The woman thanked me, and we swapped a handful more pleasantries – I explained that I, too, had been a single mother with two boys – before they went home, and I went back to my near-empty sandwich station.

I spent the rest of the evening thinking of the dead girls' mothers; Lucy's mother, with some emphasis. In bed that night the same thought chased its own tail around my mind like a dog set on tearing itself apart: *Because I'm in a position to, because I'm in a position to...*

FOURTEEN

I had made a tremendous effort. But I didn't want it to look like I had. That morning, wearing a slim-fitting black skirt, a mustard blouse, kitten heels and opaque tights, I opened the front door to Kitsell. He looked taken aback but didn't say anything. Instead I offered an excuse for the obvious work I'd put into my appearance that day: 'I have to go into the agency office for a meeting this afternoon and I didn't want to come home and change.' He nodded and said he understood. Thompson was less understanding when I climbed into the front passenger seat of the car.

'He isn't worth the lipstick, Maggie.'

'It isn't for him,' I snapped back.

Petulant and scorned, I spent the short journey to the prison staring out of the window like a teenager who'd been reprimanded for wearing blush on her cheeks. Kitsell spoke to me from the back of the car about some of Rule's points of interest, namely why Edward had thought to mention the Brighton trip at all.

'I honestly don't know,' I answered.

'And no one is doubting that, Maggie, but it would be a good thing to push.'

'Okay.'

But I didn't want to push. Pushing might mean uncovering something that was best left heavy beneath mounds of earth. Since I'd spoken to Finn about that first meeting with Edward, I had searched and scoured through pictures to find some clue of the significance of Brighton already. The only thing I could remember with some certainty was that yes, Edward had taken a fall during that trip. He was forever falling though. 'You're too clumsy to be a runner,' I'd joked with him once and he'd only patted his flattened stomach and smiled. He so often worried about inheriting his father's enthusiasm for pale ale and a lack of exercise, as though either thing could be shared through a genetic strand.

'But we'll take what we can get, won't we, Kitsell?' Thompson adopted a softer tone then, as though to be reassuring. Though his uncharacteristic efforts at reassurance so often went towards unsettling me further. 'Rule will take what she can get as well.' It sounded more like a command or an instruction, rather than an innocent statement. And I worried whether ill words had already been passed between the old and the new worker bees on Edward's case. I wanted to ask, part through curiosity but so much through sheer nosiness, and I worked especially hard to stifle that urge. I still hadn't forgiven his lipstick remark, and I resolved to limit myself to small talk and murmurings.

Rule was waiting outside of the prison when we arrived. She cooed the same and similar comments that Kitsell had already shared, stressing the importance of the holiday, why Brighton, why this, why–

'I can follow basic instructions,' I snapped when she was halfway through... something, 'I've been coached well enough during the car journey here, thank you, detective. I'd just like to press on with it all now, please.'

She looked taken aback, and I wondered how often – or not – people answered her instructions with such a bite. 'Of course.'

Rule led the way through the prison, back to the twinned rooms at its heart. Edward wasn't there yet. But no sooner had I said hello to Newell – who was kind enough *not* to give me a chapter and verse reminder of my instructions for the day – and the back door eased open. Edward looked different today, not in a complimentary way either. His complexion had yellowed and his eyes sunk, dropping into his sallow face that looked marred by a lack of sleep. But when he sat at the table I noticed him wince; he made an effort to clutch at his side but soon found that the handcuffs inhibited him. It was so unusual to see Edward in pain. Like muscle memory, I wondered where it was, what was the cause, whether there was anything I could do to soothe the ill. I watched him, all the while I was pulling in and expelling hearty breaths, as though stifling an urge to vomit, and I encouraged the feeling to pass. I couldn't step in the room until it had.

'You're free to go in whenever you're ready,' Rule said from somewhere behind me.

'I know,' I answered, 'but I'll feel better for making him wait.'

Edward couldn't keep still throughout our talking. The chairs in the room were metal, hard and cold, and I imagined that couldn't be especially comfortable against whatever pain he was fighting. Nevertheless, he managed to remember details from the holiday that I had long ago forgotten. Otis had fallen on some rocks while trying to get as close as possible to what he thought was a sea cave; I had bought a floral print dress one day and a thick, roll-necked jumper the next because the weather had been so changeable over the time we were there; Finn had cried when we had run out of two-pence pieces to put in the arcade slot machines, because there was a toy *so* close to the edge.

'Would have been cheaper to just buy him a bloody toy,' Edward joked.

But we hadn't. Instead, Edward had changed up another pound coin and he and Finn had persisted, until the small lump of plastic had tumbled through the open mouth of the machine. Shortly afterwards Edward had given Otis another pound coin to do with as he pleased, because we never gave one without the other.

'You seem to remember a lot from that holiday.'

Edward narrowed his eyes at my observation. 'We had some corkers over the years.' He leaned forwards as he had done the last time, lessening the distance across the table. I could smell something on him; it was clinical, medicinal. 'Do you remember the time we went to Wales and–'

'I'm not sure I'm finished talking about Brighton.'

Edward side-glanced to the two-way mirror in the room and then back to me. 'You mean they're not finished with us talking about Brighton?'

'Do you remember falling over, when you went for a run?'

Edward thinned his lips and shook his head in answer.

'Finn remembered it before I did.'

He smiled then. 'You spoke to Finn about me?'

'Mm,' I murmured, 'he sends his best.'

The smile widened again. 'Really?'

'No, Edward, not really.'

The contented expression fell in a single movement. Edward dropped back in his chair then, and stared at his cuffed hands. 'I know you don't want to be doing this, Maggie, but you don't have to be cruel with it.'

'Oh, I'm sorry,' my tone was jovial, mocking; it surprised me. 'Does it hurt your feelings to know the children you abandoned, for a life of murder and mayhem, don't want anything to do with you? They have lives, Edward. They're young men now and–'

'Don't you think I know that?' He slammed both hands hard against the table as though to punctuate his point and I flinched. 'I know that I've lost my sons all because of those bitches. I lost my wife to them, too.'

Those bitches. It echoed around my head as though shouted into a cavern. I felt a belch rise in me that I thought would bring sickness with it, and I pressed my hand to my lips to stifle the feeling. In the dead seconds that followed, I was desperate for Rule, Kitsell, *anyone* to burst into the room and halt the interview. When it became uncomfortably clear that that wasn't going to happen, I felt around for something to say in answer.

'It sounds like you're blaming *them* for what happened.'

Edward looked up at the ceiling. 'Some of those women...' He shook his head and seemed to think better of speaking aloud whatever the end of the sentence was. When he looked back at me, his expression had steeled; his eyes were darker than they had been minutes before, I was convinced of it. 'Nothing happened in Brighton. I pinky-swear it.' He made an effort to hold out a hand to me, his smallest finger raised in promise. I felt my skin prickle at the thought of contact with him. 'Can you even remember the last time you touched me, Maggie?'

And of course, I could. It was the morning the police came. Edward had left for work already and I was tending to the boys, both of whom happened to be at home with a stomach bug. The house was a mess of soiled things and half-eaten pieces of toast. Both of the children were parked in front of the television in the living room, huddled beneath so many blankets that I thought it had constituted a fort. Edward had asked me over our breakfast whether I needed for him to take the day off, to help. He was so often doing that, so often trying to be more and more involved with the children. It had been one of my favourite things about him since fatherhood had struck him. But I'd shaken away the offer. Instead, I had seen him to the door with his suit jacket and his briefcase, and handed them both over to him as though I were a Stepford creature. And then I had stretched up onto my tiptoes, such was our height difference, and given my husband one long, last kiss.

Kitsell and Thompson had arrived twenty minutes later.

'No,' I answered, and he sighed.

'Well, pinky or not, nothing happened in–' His sentence broke off into a cry and he clutched at his side again as I'd seen him do earlier.

Do not ask if he's okay, I coached myself, *do not ask if he's okay*.

He forced a long breath out. 'I think that's us done for the day, Mags.'

'I still need to know about Brighton.'

Edward nodded towards the mirror. 'Let them work it out. Can someone get me out of here, please? Some drugs would be nice, while you're at it.' He shouted the instruction into the room, knowing the speakers, the cameras, the onlookers would all hear him.

There was a long pause while we both waited for something to happen. When nothing did, my curiosity bit into me like a rabid dog.

'Is it the cancer?'

'Nah,' he rubbed at his side again, 'that's where I keep my conscience.'

'I wasn't aware you still had one.'

Edward looked amused by that. 'You're a lot sharper than you used to be.'

'Well, life makes you brittle.'

'I can understand that.' He fidgeted in his seat again and glanced at the doorway, in anticipation, readiness. But the guards weren't rushing. 'I do feel bad about some things, Maggie, you must know that,' he said in a lowered voice. It didn't matter how quiet he spoke, though, the small voice recorder between us was still documenting everything we shared. 'What I put you through, I feel terrible still about that, and the boys. None of you...' He petered out as the door clanged open behind him. I wondered whether the guard had had to consult with the likes of Rule before coming in to yank Edward out.

'Come on, then, O'Connor, let's be having you.'

'Let's do this again soon, eh?' Edward winked at me as he struggled to stand up. 'Give my love to the boys if they can stomach it.'

I stayed mute while he and his minder trod to the door.

'Maggie,' he managed to turn and I saw that same shark smile, 'have a think about Nottingham. Before the boys' time, wasn't it? Good times, good times...' he said over and again until the door closed and the sound of him died.

FIFTEEN

The downstairs bathroom was typically reserved for guests. But I hadn't thought I could make it to the upstairs one. My knees were pressed hard into the cold of the tiles, and my hands clutched at the rim of the toilet seat to keep me steady – or close to steady. I hadn't managed dinner last night or breakfast this morning. The only thing my body was able to fetch back was cold coffee that burnt my throat on its leave. But undeterred by the lack of food in my stomach, I had been desperate to expel something, to purge, somehow. When I had managed to count out thirty seconds without a stomach spasm I reached up to flush the toilet, and then struggled to turn and sit properly, my back against the wall. I waited another thirty seconds before I moved again, this time to a standing position. I splashed my face with cool water and cupped in a mouthful that I swilled with and then spat back into the basin. There was a lingering furriness in the walls of my cheeks, moss and lichen blooming in place of saliva.

Kitsell, Thompson and Rule were talking among themselves in the living room when I trod back in. I took slow movements, conscious of upsetting the apple cart of my insides. There was a glass of water on the coffee table that I thought hadn't been there before.

'I thought you might need it,' Rule said, when she noticed my stare. It was her first time in my home, and this wasn't the impression I had been hoping to make. Not that she was a conventional guest here, but still, I thought there was likely some social etiquette against rushing from a gathering of visitors to upchuck in the next room.

'Thank you,' I managed.

Alongside the water there was the picture still. None of them had seen fit to move it. Kitsell reached forward then, to clutch it between finger and thumb, and offered it to me a second time. I took it from him and stared, searching for something that I might recognise.

'There's *nothing* familiar about this woman?' Thompson pushed.

I shook my head. 'There really isn't. I'm so sorry,' I offered without knowing what I was apologising for. I knew they were asking about this woman for a reason though, in hopes that I might help them, somehow. Even though I'd hardly helped them at all to date – or at least that's how it felt. 'Who is she?' I finally asked.

'Molly Quebec,' Rule answered. But she didn't offer anything more. And in the quiet space of the room suddenly a jigsaw began falling into place; its edges didn't fit neatly and its contents were watercolour, but it was clear enough.

'She's dead, isn't she?' I asked.

I looked up in time to catch Rule glance across to Kitsell and Thompson, as though nominating one or both of them to take up the mantle of speaking. I wondered whether they'd played rock, paper, scissors between themselves in the car journey from their station to my home.

Kitsell cleared his throat and inched forwards in his seat. 'Yes.'

'Brighton,' Thompson added.

And I felt the roar of my stomach again.

'Oh God...' A strangled sound followed out of me. I didn't cry, though I felt a dam of something burst in me somewhere. I would shower when they left, I would shower and bathe and I would sob my broken heart out and–

'Maggie?' Kitsell reached over to touch my knee, as though physically pulling me back into the room. 'We've done some digging, around the time you and Edward, and the boys,' it looked a struggle for him to add that final detail, 'around the time you were all there. Molly was found– It was toward the tail-end of your holiday, Maggie. She was found in a woodland area.' He paused and inhaled deeply then. I heard his breath shake. 'It's a popular area with runners, apparently. Or at least it was, then. They never– There were never any leads, on who might have done it. The police...' He petered out and shook his head. Rule stepped in to help him and I afforded her a Brownie point.

'The police wrapped it as a cold case some time ago. But we're now looking at connections between this girl and Edward. We know whereabouts she was staying. What we're trying to determine is whether they would have met beforehand, on any occasion, or whether... whether Edward– If it was opportunistic.'

It was too much. Someone flicked a faucet to full power and I felt water rush between my ears, swallowing any further sounds. Everyone seemed to be quiet for too long a time.

Rule nudged the glass of water towards me. 'You should sip at this.'

'Do you have any brandy?' Thompson asked then, and Kitsell guffawed at the question.

'It's half ten in the morning.'

'She's had a shock,' Thompson snapped back.

'I don't think brandy will help,' I managed.

From the corner of my eye I saw Rule nod along. 'Do you need just a minute?'

'I'm not sure a minute will help either.' I reached forward and turned the girl's picture over. She lay face down on the table and I wondered whether that's how she'd been when they found her. 'What happened to her, to the girl?' I asked then, trying to stifle the life out of the thought; the accompanying imaginings that flooded in with it.

'Maggie, I–'

'I need to know,' I interrupted Kitsell. I had no interest in his kid gloves then. Something had been worn inside me, emotionally, psychically even. I wanted someone to pour salt in the wound, bury their fingers in it to see how far down the cut went. It felt like a form of self-harm.

Rule cleared her throat. 'She was badly beaten, perimortem. There were a lot of bruises, cuts, scrapes, that sort of thing. There were fractures to her face from the beating, too,' she swallowed hard and a low gulp echoed out of her, 'her lower jaw was fractured, as well as one of her cheekbones.'

She paused for too long then so I pushed. 'And?'

'And then she was strangled.'

'Was there– Did she have any signs of–'

'No, there weren't any signs of sexual assault.'

I nodded and managed to force out a long breath. *That sounds like Edward,* I thought as though he were a thoughtful husband coming home with a surprise bunch of flowers. *That sounds like my Edward.* It had been a small saving grace that there had never been signs of sexual assault on the bodies of the local women. It would have made it harder, for everyone. I'd hardly handled twenty years of knowing my husband was a murderer; to think of him as something worse would have been too much for my human heart to bear. Though of course, if this girl was murdered when we were in Brighton, then that would mean–

'This,' I tapped the table where the picture was face down, 'this was so much earlier than the other murders. Edward, he didn't start– He didn't do what he did until much later. This can't have been...' I petered out when I saw their expressions. *But of course, it could have been*, I realised then. I reached for the glass of water with a hand that still shook like an autumnal leaf in a strong breeze; I was worried I might spill the drink, but my mouth was too dry to talk any further – and I had questions. 'You think he's been doing this for years, don't you? Years longer than– A much longer time than...'

'Maggie, I'm sorry,' Kitsell answered without really answering. 'There has always been the possibility that Edward may have killed women before killing locally. We knew that.'

But they hadn't *known* it. They had only *thought* it. Edward had been methodical here, choosing young women with active social lives, loose family structures; young women who might feasibly be off the grid for a day or two, with friends or with work. The thought that had gone into choosing them, discarding of them, it had seemed, they told me, like a practised hand; someone who knew what they were doing. That hadn't been true until now.

'What do you need from me?'

'What records do you have of family holidays?'

I smiled but the expression strained my face. 'Photo albums, so many photo albums.'

They had, up until only thirty minutes ago, been filled with happy memories. Eating ice cream in Weston-super-Mare; attending the carnival in Taunton; city breaks, once or twice, without the children, though I'd always felt guilty for leaving them behind. And that's when another thought struck.

'Why do you think it's only family holidays?'

Rule thinned her lips. 'It's a starting point. There's the possibility that when Edward was away on work trips, that he also took that as an opportunity. That's something we'll need to explore further down the line, as these new cases develop and advance.'

I shook my head; that hadn't been what I was asking. 'No, why do you think it's only *family* holidays?' I said again, changing my emphasis. I looked between the detectives hoping they might catch at my meaning, hoping, truly, that I wouldn't have to voice the worry aloud. But not even Thompson looked to gauge what I was asking. 'If he started earlier than everyone thought, could he not have started earlier again? Could he not have been doing this...' *For our entire lives together.* And I remembered then how Edward had mentioned Nottingham; a trip that predated the boys.

Kitsell looked genuinely saddened by the question. 'That's another possibility we'll have to explore at some point, depending on the information that Edward can provide us with in the coming meetings.'

'Assuming you feel comfortable with further meetings,' Thompson added. I didn't know whether he was saying it from kindness or duty. Either way, I was glad to have been presented with an escape hatch.

'If you're able to look back through those albums, Maggie.' Rule spoke again then, and I noted that she hadn't given me breathing space enough to answer Thompson's implied offer. 'If you can look back through them and note down locations, dates, if there's anything at all that jumps out at you from memories of those holidays, all of that would be especially helpful to have at this point. It gives us avenues to start investigating, whether Edward is forthcoming with information or not.'

I nodded. 'Of course.' The boys might remember more, or remember differently, but it was an ask that I wasn't prepared to extend to them. Otis and I still hadn't spoken. 'May I ask Edward about them? If there are things, memories that come back. Is pushing him...'

'Pushing him is perfectly fine with us,' she answered.

'Providing you feel comfortable with that,' Thompson added.

There was nothing comfortable about any of this, I wanted to remind them. But the discomfort was part of the penance. I had to be doing something; I had to know what my husband had done.

SIXTEEN

I had requested permission – a child approaching their parents – to take the full photo albums in with me. 'He wants to shit on these, so let him,' had been my explanation when Rule asked whether it was entirely necessary to take *every* photo album I had been able to lay my hands on in the two days that had passed since the detectives' visit to my home. Though I soon established that some of her reluctance was nothing at all to do with whether it was 'necessary' or not, and everything to do with the hoop-jumping that would have been involved at the prison had I arrived with binders upon binders of still images to throw at Edward. They would have all needed to be thoroughly checked, lest I smuggle in a sheet of pills or a razor blade. To sidestep the lengthy process that that endeavour would have caused, I spent an entire night choosing *one* photograph from every location that I could place inside the albums. I'd had no idea that we'd been on quite so many family holidays over the years, even if they were sometimes only weekends away rather than extended stays anywhere. There were some images filed away that denoted holidays Edward and I had shared before the boys, too. The echo of Kitsell – 'That's another possibility we'll have to explore at some point' – sang out in the back of my mind.

I filed away the images I had chosen in a large white envelope – easy for an inspecting guard to tip out and search – and everything else I had relegated back to the cave of my spare bedroom. The curtains were pulled, the albums themselves stashed beneath a bed that had never been slept in; though I'd optimistically bought it in case one of the boys might stay over with a partner one night. When I pulled the door closed behind me it felt like locking a tomb, which was nothing short of what those memories deserved now, as far as I was concerned.

Rule collected me from the house that day. I spent the journey to the prison in the front passenger seat of her car, clutching the envelope to me as though it contained answers to a test, or a sequence of winning lottery numbers.

'How are the boys handling all of this?' she asked, quite out of nowhere, when we found ourselves stuck behind a string of unmoving cars at some temporary traffic lights. It was the first time she'd acknowledged my children.

'They're not,' I answered plainly. 'Finn, the last time I saw him, was tetchy... if that's even the right word, about what his father might admit to. He doesn't remember everything, well, anything much at all, from the first time around. I think, for him, this may as well be Edward's first wave of confession.' I pulled in a shaky breath before I continued. 'Otis hasn't spoken to me since I told him that I'd be seeing his father.'

'I see.' She craned her neck to try to get a better view of the cars in front. 'That can't be a particularly helpful reaction for you, when you're trying to do something good here.'

'Is it good?' I snapped. 'These women, they've been gone for so long, their families have mourned. I understand Lucy, why people would want to know about Lucy, but these,' I gestured with the envelope, 'is it good to be excavating these?'

Rule took a long time to answer. She rolled the car forward as the lights changed and changed again, and we found ourselves closer to the brim of the traffic's end.

'I couldn't live with not knowing what had happened to one of my girls,' she admitted. 'It wouldn't matter how much time had passed, how much I thought I'd managed to grieve, I couldn't live with the not knowing about who had taken them, and why.'

'What if there isn't a why?'

She sighed. 'Sometimes there isn't.' She knocked the car into first gear and moved forwards through the lights. 'But there's always a who, and that's worth knowing.'

Neither of us said anything more on the journey after that. What was there to say? While I watched the city blur into its outer limits, I realised that she was, of course, entirely right. If I didn't know what had happened to one of the boys then it would be a living grief; something that tore through me and nested in me and– I pushed out a stream of air. She was right, I told myself again, and that was the only grab rail I could find to hang on to.

Kitsell and Thompson were waiting outside the prison with Newell. It was the youngest of the three that looked to be talking in a hurried and animated fashion. Newell flung his arms out as he spoke, then one hand flew to his temple and kneaded the skin there.

'We're off to a good start,' Rule said as she yanked the handbrake on. No sooner was she out of the car and she was already shouting across to her junior to ask what was happening. 'Has there been a cock-up?'

'Not a cock-up, per se,' Thompson answered with a raised eyebrow.

'It isn't a cock-up,' Newell answered then, 'but apparently Edward had a rough night last night, health reasons, medication reasons, fuck knows. But there's going to be a delay in bringing him through today. Doctor's orders, apparently.'

Rule nodded, thought for a moment and then said, 'I don't care.'

Newell looked taken aback. 'With the greatest of respect–'

'Nothing anyone ever says after that is respectful,' Rule interrupted, 'you can house that phrase in the same box as "no offence, but…" the next time you're catching up on your admin. We're here to see Edward and we'll see him. Maggie isn't being kept waiting.'

Newell laughed; a huff of a laugh, tinged with relief. 'I'm so glad you're here.'

'Come on, let's be having him…'

It wasn't until the duty guard was flicking through my photograph selection that anyone spoke again, and it was Kitsell who broke the silence.

'Sorting through those can't have been easy.'

'No…' I watched as the memories flicked through before my eyes like a shoddily produced picture book. 'But it doesn't matter whether it's easy for me, does it?' When he didn't respond I turned to catch a side-on look at him. 'No, it doesn't,' I answered for him, 'this isn't meant to be easy for me.'

Where last time I had asked for Edward to wait – for Edward to be made to wait, rather – this time I wanted to be the first one in the room. I set the recorder on the corner of the table but then trod around to Edward's side, and I allowed myself a strategic minute or two to lay out the many photos I had stripped from our family albums: Brighton; Bournemouth; Torquay; the boys; me with the boys; the boys with Edward, where one of them in their teenage rage – most likely Otis – had taken to scratching

Edward's eyes out of the image. If anything, though, it had given him more of a demonic feel than staring into his dark eyes might have done ordinarily. When I was pleased with their layout, I nodded to the two-way mirror to let Rule know I was ready. And then I waited – one leg folded over the other, my hands tucked neatly together and resting on the table.

Edward didn't look sick at all. While during our last visit he may have looked pained, compromised somehow by twinges throughout his failing body, this time, anyone could be forgiven for thinking there was nothing ailing him at all. I wanted signs of the cancer; I wanted to be able to see it working. But instead he only smirked as he entered the room and saw the display waiting for him – there was no discomfort, even though I was chronically desperate for it. He landed heavily in the chair, thanked the guard with a tone of politeness and familiarity that I hated, and then scanned the images.

'Are we having a show and tell?'

'Good idea,' I leaned back in my chair, 'I'll show you a picture of a place we visited with our children, and you can tell me whether you murdered someone there.' I was glad that my voice hadn't shaken; I had been practising the sentence in front of the mirror all morning, and the relief of making it through word-perfect pulsed in me. 'How does that sound?'

'I told you nothing happened in Brighton.'

'And I'm telling you, I think you're a liar.' I let a silence swell. 'Who's Molly Quebec?'

Edward looked so puzzled that it crossed my mind, only for a moment, that perhaps he really wasn't anything to do with that murder. But then a counter-thought gripped me at the throat and dug its teeth in: *Did he have time to get her name?*

'She was murdered in Brighton, when we were there with the boys.'

Edward narrowed his eyes. 'Funny coincidence.'

'I've never believed in those.'

'Ah, well now you're the liar,' he said in a playful tone. 'Do you remember the time–'

I slammed the full weight of one hand against the table. My palm slapped against the metal, and a heat spread through my skin, but I would not, could not react to it. 'Don't fucking goad me into talking about our life, Edward.' I had never been a curse-word person. The F-word felt strange in my mouth. For years, I had reprimanded the boys whenever they used it under my roof, even into their adulthood. But somehow, now, it felt like the force I needed.

'Maggie...' He leaned back in his chair to widen the distance between us, as though I were the dangerous one out of the two of us. 'That temper isn't yours.'

'You don't know me anymore, Ed. You don't know me, you don't know the boys, you only know murder and this place,' I looked disdainfully at the room around us, 'you only know rot, which is exactly what you deserve. But doesn't Lucy deserve better? Isn't that the whole point in this deathbed confession, or are you just fucking around to kill time?'

The floodgates had been opened. After using the word once and in fury, I could already appreciate that there were occasions when another word simply wouldn't do.

'I'm not talking about Lucy.'

'Then talk to me about Molly.'

'I don't know anyone called Molly!'

I lifted the picture of the boys and their sun-red skin on Brighton beach. Underneath, there was the picture I'd been shown of Molly days ago; the face I hadn't been able to shake seeing. When they'd asked if I recognised her, I'd sincerely answered, 'No.'

Edward's expression gave him away so quickly, though, that

there was no opportunity for him to lie, or even feign ignorance. Instead he only nodded. 'Oh.'

My stomach turned over; a wave trapped inside, thrashing at the walls.

'How many were there, Edward, really? Do you even know?'

Edward tilted his head from one side to the other and back again, as though doing mental arithmetic. That was always his forte with the boys; he took charge of maths and science while I took charge of English and languages. It was the only part of our household that saw a fair division of labour.

'Honestly, Maggie, I don't know what to tell you.'

'Do you know how many?' I pushed, and he only shrugged.

'No.'

SEVENTEEN

Two Christmases ago, the boys had bought me – among other soft and soothing things – a dressing gown with a fleece lining. I'd had the same one for years by then, but I could never bring myself to take this pale pink and floral-patterned replacement out of the plastic sleeve it had arrived in. Now, I was into my third day of wearing it. I had been screening phone calls from friends and police officials alike. My to-do list for work was finally being whittled down, the distraction of those ongoing projects being the only thing that eased my ill feelings for a while. All it took, though, was five minutes away from my kitchen table to boil the kettle, to fetch another rice cake, to use the bathroom, and the badness flooded back like a bath left running for too long; it overflowed in tears, and glugging sounds as I tried to catch my breath.

In those hollow moments when I wasn't working, all I could think about was the countless women. And now, of course, they were literally countless. The number nine had regained its neutral standing after so many years of feeling cursed for me. Now, the curse was infinity; it was the algebraic X that I couldn't find the value of.

When the to-do list had finally worn through me, and I found my eyes could no longer stand to look at my laptop screen, I withdrew from the kitchen and took myself to the living room instead. I tucked as much of my body as I could into the small hold of the armchair and tipped my head back to rest. But when I closed my eyes all I saw was Edward's shrug; his near pride in admitting that no, he couldn't remember them all. And whether the comparison was right or wrong, I couldn't stop myself from wondering whether this was how the wives of serial adulterers might feel: the endless tallying of nights when he *might* have been with someone else; occasions when a scorned wife was now *sure* he had been doing something he shouldn't have been.

'I think I would prefer it,' I said aloud to no one. My voice cracked around the words. I tried to place the last time I'd spoken. *Was it really at the prison?* I thought, knowing there must have been words shared on the journey home, too, surely. But the horror of that last visit had blotted out anything that came immediately after it. Trauma will do that.

I pulled my phone free from the pocket of my fleece and thumbed into my most recent calls. They were all from Kitsell or Rule. There was no sign of the boys there; no sign of Bernie. Anyone looking at my phone could be forgiven for believing that my life did not exist too much outside of amateur detective work. And maybe they'd be right. Though it felt altogether less noble, and certainly less wanted, than the likes of Miss Marple's endeavours. Besides which, in this scenario I needed to be both detective figure and jilted wife; it felt like a recipe for rage, and I only wished that was the right word for what I'd been feeling.

In my contacts list I scrolled down to Otis's number before scrolling back up to Finn's. Otis had made his feelings clear in all this and drawing him into the sting of his father's admission was unlikely to help. Meanwhile, Finn had been kind, gentle the other week when he'd brought food and discussion to my home. But he also hadn't called since, nor had they replied to my text messages, either of them.

'They don't care about you anymore,' I told the phone screen before shaking the thought away. It was unreasonable to accuse them of that. *But the evidence suggests...*

If I were to call Bernie, I suspected she wouldn't even answer. We were outside of our allotted monthly catch-up, and the last time I had broken that agreement was to talk to her about Edward. Once bitten, I couldn't imagine that she might walk into such a conversation for a second time. I longed for my mother to be alive then. She didn't know that I knew, but my father had cheated on her once; I know because I saw him with the other woman. I don't know how my mother put a stop to it, or even when, but she had. And when I had told her of my plans to marry Edward – 'You can do better than him, my darling girl, you can' – she had taken me to one side when Dad was busying himself elsewhere, and she had told me about men and their wandering and their cheating. 'Christ, they don't half cheat,' she'd said. She also said I should never stand for it.

I'd naively told her Edward wasn't like that.

And look at where that untruth has gotten you...

I had to remind myself that no, Edward had not committed infidelity – in the strictest and most literal sense of the word, he had not. I couldn't relegate his behaviour to, 'He was with her when he should have been home with me,' because his not being at home with me may have saved my life. It was a horrid thought that had emerged from the murky waters of my mind repeatedly over the years: *Why them? Why not me?* Now, likening myself to a Victorian housewife treated so foully by her spouse, the thought stirred again. And again I had to remind myself that he was not sleeping with these women. Edward's crime had never been sexual, in fact, only violent so–

Never been sexual that you know of.

The thought came in someone else's voice and with it there rose bile and bitterness in the back of my throat. For the second time in as many weeks I rushed to the guest bathroom downstairs and threw myself onto my knees, my head bent over the bowl of the toilet and my hands clasped ahead of me. I wondered whether this purging might double as an act of contrition.

With the back of one hand I wiped my mouth clean and with the other I reached up towards the sink, grabbing its edge to heave myself upright. I looked in the mirror and saw an aged hag staring back. There was nothing of my mother in me, nor my father. Bernie had borrowed from both of their appearances: Dad's nose; Mum's smile. I had forever been a type of black sheep in my otherwise normal family. But all I needed, all I truly longed for then, was a way in which to feel close to them all.

The house where Bernie and I grew up was a two-hour drive away. Mum and Dad were buried in the cemetery local to the house. It was the first excuse I'd had in days to wear actual clothes, but even the rub of denim against my legs felt too harsh. Every time I pressed the clutch the fabric caught against my knee, the green wire of a washing-up sponge. I listened to the radio on the journey. It had been nearly an hour and a half when a news report cut in; when they mentioned Edward, I changed to another station. Nothing made me feel my age like listening to, and trying to place, contemporary and popular music, anything that might be in the charts now. *Though the charts aren't what they used to be*, I thought as another radio presenter burst in with an outro for So-and-So and their new track What's-It-Called. But it was better than hearing about Edward.

The story of his new – *old?* – crimes hadn't broken yet, but there were murmurings of it. The local newspaper headlines had already announced 'Close Friend of Killer Helping Police'. I resented having been relegated to the status of a close friend, a close anything, of Edward's. Though of course, I preferred that lie, and the anonymity it afforded me, over the truth of what was happening. In the dead of night I'd started to fantasise about local journalists huddled around Edward's past, trying to determine the name of the person they were looking for. It was nothing short of a miracle that they hadn't arrived at my front door yet. I suspected it was only a matter of time, though, now there were whispers of a helping hand in the investigation, and in my darkest moments I almost wished for the reveal, if only to finally get it out of the way.

When I was close to the cemetery I turned the radio off entirely. It felt disrespectful to pull into the car park with the hammer and nail of a modern-day baseline echoing out from the car. Though there wasn't anyone to hear it even; the car park was barren. It was raining hard, admittedly, and they'd forecast more rain, and even a deep freeze for the coming days. It wasn't ideal weather for trudging through a grassed and now muddy landscape in search of a loved one's headstone. I was willing to take my chances in going home with dirtied shoes though, if it meant seeing Mum and Dad.

They were buried together – or rather, their ashes were. For their differences and their spats, they had always told us both that when the end came, they wanted to up their chances of togetherness going into whatever afterlife might be waiting for them. Dad went first; a heart attack, brought on from years of smoking and essentially gargling with frying oils. Mum went shortly afterwards; there was nothing wrong with her, they said, nothing they could determine, only a broken heart. She slipped away while no one was watching one evening; even the hospital staff took their time in noticing. I had sat outside her room and wept and a man, who looked tired and teared himself, rubbed my shoulder like he knew me.

'Someone told me once that this must be hell,' he'd said without looking at me. But I looked at him, stared hard to find trace of religion or anything else that I could have lived without in those moments. 'This must be hell,' he'd said again, 'and once we've been through hell, we get to something better.'

I nodded, even though I took no comfort in what he'd said.

'I'm sorry for your loss,' he'd added then, and I wanted to ask how he knew.

Mum and Dad's shared stone was bare. I laid down the yellow roses I had stopped to buy on the way. They were Mum's favourite. I don't know that Dad would have had a favourite flower to speak of, but it also didn't feel right to set down a packet of Lambert & Butler for him either. I knelt in a muddy patch in front of their stone. It didn't matter; some things can be washed out, I reminded myself. I'd worried that I might embarrass myself by crying when I got here – Mum had always hated it when I cried – but instead I felt a wash of quiet move over me. This closeness was all I'd needed.

'I do miss you both,' I told them. 'I need someone who–'

The shrill ring of my phone in my pocket cut my sentence in half. I thought of not answering, for two reasons. The first being that rain was pelting hard against me still, and I wasn't sure modern technology could handle those elements. The second being I truly, deeply didn't want to speak to anyone. But when you're a parent, ignoring phone calls becomes harder. *What if it's one of the boys?* I couldn't stop myself from thinking, even though in my bones I knew it was unlikely.

When I pulled the phone out and saw the name – Kitsell – I

felt even less like answering. I always visited the grave during the evening, when the world was at its quietest. The phone call was a harsh interruption to that. And at this time of night, Kitsell couldn't be calling with good news; assuming there was any good news to be had at all in this situation. Still, my morals got the better of me.

'Hello?'

'Maggie, it's me. How are you doing?'

This was the first time we'd spoken since my last meeting with Edward. I wanted to believe that he was calling only to ask whether I was okay. I couldn't quite marry myself to that reality though. 'What does he want now?' I asked.

Kitsell sighed. 'He's asked to see you again, sooner rather than later. Would you...'

He didn't want to ask, of course, which is why his sentence had curled over at its end. I knew what was being asked, or expected of me, though. I looked to Mum and Dad for an answer and tried to place what their advice might be, if they were still here to provide me with it. And after some thought, I pulled in the deepest breath I could manage against the cooling temperatures and answered him as plainly as I could.

'No.'

It had been ten days since the call from Kitsell. For the first time in weeks I had managed what felt like a full night's sleep and I couldn't decide whether it was enforced rest, from sheer exhaustion, or whether it was something to do with the half a bottle of wine I'd had with Rebecca the evening before. It hadn't been until halfway through the evening that I'd started to remember how nice it could be to be in the company of others, and I was thankful for her last-minute suggestion of a takeaway – she brought Chinese to my house – and a few glasses of wine to ring in my birthday. She had told me about her goings-on in life of late and I had shared some, but obviously not all, of mine. Rebecca had been given the highlights reel of writing assignments I'd accepted, work I was making a bid for, and my utter relief and immeasurable joy that the boys had suggested dinner out somewhere to celebrate my birthday as a family. I'd extended invitations to Emilia and Alice, and Finn had replied to say he'd see what he could do.

'It's the least you deserve,' Rebecca had said when I'd told her of their plan. Though I wasn't sure I deserved it in the slightest. In fact, up until hearing from Finn the afternoon before, I'd been planning to spend my birthday cooking and its evening at the food bank. The guilt that surged through me at having abandoned those plans due to a better offer was unexpected, but undeniable.

I'd reached a compromise with myself that I would still spend the day cooking. But instead of attending the food bank itself, I'd texted Claire to ask whether she might be able to collect some home-cooked meals from me in the afternoon. She had replied to ask whether three (ish) would be okay and although I hated that ambiguity I'd answered to say it was fine. I spent my birthday morning peeling and chopping vegetables, browning meat, and laying pasta sheets. There were two large lasagnes and one shepherd's pie in the oven before midday had rolled around, which would give them reasonable time to cool, too.

'This is as good as it gets then,' I said to no one as I waited for the kettle to boil. I dropped a slice of bread into the toaster, too. If the boys were taking me for dinner, the least I could do was make sure I had the stomach for it. I busied myself with turning on my laptop and arranging my work to-do list for the day. I scrunched up the cooking to-do list and threw it into the bin on my way back to the counter, where I made a cup of tea strong enough to be considered "cedar" on a paint chart. One of my work assignments at the time was a series of presentations on painting and decorating for a college down south; where the teachers were apparently capable of teaching, but incapable of writing their own materials.

'Those who can't...' I mumbled as I sat down at the kitchen table. Then berated myself for the judgement. I knew then that I would need to be as kind as possible to anyone who might cross my path today. If I was to earn my birthday meal out with my boys, I had to assuage my guilt at all costs.

But I drew the line at answering my phone when Kitsell

called me at lunchtime. Edward would not be allowed to ruin this day...

I wore my best black dress. It was high-necked and long-sleeved, with a ribbon that tied around the waist. I hadn't weighed myself in years, but from its fit I knew that I needed to make a greater effort with food. I hoped the boys wouldn't notice. Though given how often I wore anything fitted, against jeans and oversized jumpers, it was an unlikely thing for either of them to see. My hair was too dry and wild to leave down, so I used a large tortoiseshell grip to hold it in place and I pinned the wild strands as best as I could. It had been a long time since I had looked in a mirror and felt attractive. But at the very least, I thought that evening I looked okay, neat. And certainly presentable enough to be spending the night with my sons and their partners, who had agreed to come along to dinner.

I drove myself there, owing to the limited space in Otis's car, and when I arrived at Benedicto's – a restaurant I had to use my navigation system to find – I was touched by the effort the boys had clearly made. This wasn't a high-street chain, but rather an independent bistro on the outskirts of town, with bright lights and a heaving car park. Finn had texted me during my journey to say they were already inside. So I used my rear-view to check that my minimal make-up hadn't smudged on the journey here – I was so unaccustomed to wearing it now – and then I hurried in to meet my birthday party.

I could have cried when I saw them: a huddle of helium balloons attached to the table with 'Happy birthday' printed around their domes. The boys were up and out of their seats when they saw me; Otis the first to greet me with a hug. And I wondered whether this exact moment in time counted as an olive branch.

'Happy birthday, Mum.'

'Thank you,' I answered as he pulled away. But I caught him by the hand to pull his attention back. 'Really, Otis, thank you.'

'You're my mum.' He shrugged and smiled and again I felt a rise of tears.

'Come on, don't hog the birthday girl.' Finn hugged me, too, then and as he pulled away he turned and pointed to Alice; his beautiful, beautiful Alice who was a vision in a red dress and lipstick to match. 'If you hate the balloons then you can blame her.'

'Shut up,' Alice slapped his arm playfully as she stood, 'she doesn't hate them. Who can possibly hate balloons?' She pulled me into a hug then – I couldn't remember the last time I had been touched by so many, so much and so soon – and whispered, 'You don't hate them, do you?'

I laughed. 'I think they're a beautiful touch.'

'Maggie.' Emilia leaned over the table when the first round of hugs had finished, and awkwardly tucked an arm behind my shoulders. She was beautiful, too, with her copper hair in loose curls and a black dress that looked more suited to a night on the town than it did a birthday meal with an old – *do your mid-sixties count as being old?* – mother-in-law. Her effort touched me deeply. 'Happy birthday. I'm so, so glad we can do this as a family.'

'We should honestly do stuff like this more, just anyway,' Alice added.

Their enthusiasm made me wonder why we didn't. Were the boys keeping them away from me? Were they really just *that* busy that we didn't have time for this? I wondered whether the next occasion we all sat down together would be the next birthday on the family calendar, and that thought saddened me so much that I found myself saying, 'Why don't I cook for you all this weekend?' before even checking with the boys first.

Otis glanced at Emilia, who answered for them both. 'We're actually away this weekend, I think. Is it this weekend, babe?'

'Hm,' he murmured in agreement, 'Oxford.'

'Trying to inject some culture into your diet?' Finn goaded his brother, and from there unfolded laughter, future plans and holidays that carried us through to when a waiter arrived.

'So how's everything your end, Mum? What have you done with yourself for the day?' Otis asked before taking a large sip from his lager.

I recounted my morning spent cooking and my afternoon spent doing work. 'It's been a nice, quiet birthday.'

'That food sounds delicious, by the by, so if the offer of a weekend meal is open to just the two of us...' Alice said, her tone jovial but I hoped she was being serious. 'Or you could come to ours sometime? Finn can cook.'

'I can?'

'He can?' Otis said in a mocking tone.

They didn't have time to hound each other further though. The waiter, who seemed to have only just taken our orders, soon reappeared with the beginnings of the meal. He placed pasta and pizza in front of Alice and Finn respectively, and placed a portion of garlic dough balls in the centre of the table. When he appeared for a second time he brought with him Otis's calzone, Emilia's pasta salad, and my tagliatelle. I pulled in a deep breath before I took my first bite and I tried to chew slowly, to savour the food and company at once.

'Well, happy birthday, Maggie,' Emilia said again, and she raised her glass to begin a toast. I felt rude for having started my meal already, so I rushed to swallow, grab my glass, and smile along with their happy murmurings.

Quiet followed, while everyone tucked into their meals and made appreciative noises. Alice bartered with Finn for a slice of his pizza – 'If you wanted pizza, you should have ordered pizza...' – and Emilia pulled a horrified face when presented with a mouthful of Otis's calzone to try – 'If I wanted calzone, I would have ordered...' – and I felt my stomach swell not with food, but with a kind of joy.

But like all good things, even joy can curdle when stored in improper settings.

We were edging towards having finished our dinners when an especially loud table alongside ours ordered what I thought was their third round of drinks, and started to talk about–

'Have you heard about this latest business with the O'Connor bloke?'

I stopped chewing and cast a hooded look at the boys to gauge their reactions. They were closer to the neighbouring table than I was; there was no way they hadn't heard. Otis set down his cutlery and took three thirsty mouthfuls from his drink. Finn did nothing. He reacted as though a small-scale hurricane hadn't ripped across our dining experience, as he sectioned off a chunk of garlic-stuffed crust for Alice to try. The two of them formed a bubble. Otis, I knew, would never be able to manage such a mask.

'Reckon he's finally confessing to it all.'

'Hadn't he already confessed? Like, to the nine?'

'No, no, there's *more* they're finding now.'

'Fucking hell, how many more?'

'I wish they wouldn't talk about that,' Emilia said quietly, but loud enough for me to hear. She was sitting next to me, and when I braved a look at her she flashed me a thin-lipped smile that made me wonder. 'It's just crass, isn't it?'

'What about the last girl? What's her name? Lily? Lucy?'

'Still haven't found her.'

Otis drained his drink and slammed the empty glass on the table as though to punctuate the action. 'I'm getting another, does anyone want anything?' He stood and looked to everyone but me for an answer. 'I'll just be a minute.'

When he moved away from the table there came a small crack under the weight of his second step. 'Fucking breadstick,' he explained before walking on. But I imagined the snapping sound as a break in an olive branch.

NINETEEN

I was ready to break up with Edward.

The first time I had done this, I'd followed the route of what I've heard people refer to as "ghosting". When the police took him away, his face pressed to the back window of an official vehicle like a caricature from a crime drama, it was the last time I'd spoken to him directly before all of this began. I had ignored his letters; I had refused his phone calls. Owing to the extenuating circumstances of our separating, I hadn't even needed contact with him throughout the divorce. It had crossed my mind, at the time, that he might withhold the luxury of that freedom from me, but he'd acquiesced without a question. My solicitor had passed along a message on Edward's behalf, though, to say he understood that I needed this – as though I gave a toss what Edward understood or thought.

Now, though, my concern was less about breaking up with Edward, and more rooted in my ties to Kitsell, Thompson, Rule and Newell. I'd called ahead to ask whether I could pop into the station. Kitsell had said he was glad to hear from me, and he also said that he and Thompson could visit me at home if it were more convenient. It wasn't, I explained, I wanted to see everyone. His voice became tinged then, with that quiet understanding we all have on realising that something is about to happen that we won't be pleased with, and likely will feel scuppered by. But he didn't ask any further questions; only told me the times they would be at the station, and assured me that, to the best of his knowledge, Rule and Newell would also be there. I thanked him and ended the call as quickly as I could. There was a rise of nerves in me, water coming to a boil over a hob's open flame, and I needed to find a distraction for the interim hours to make sure the pot didn't heat over.

By the time I was leaving the house my work to-do list was nearly completed, and I was sure the kitchen hadn't been so clean since the day that I'd moved in. In between work tasks, typically while waiting for the kettle to boil, I scrubbed and scoured and sprayed enough disinfectant to render the room sterile. I'd had to throw open a window eventually to let out the fumes, lest I arrive at the police station high on chemicals. Which, I decided on the long walk there, mightn't have been a bad thing.

I had hoped the walk might steady my nerves, or at the very least release more of the nervous energy that I'd been harbouring throughout the day. But when I found myself rounding the final corner, I felt an anxiety spike so severe that the back of my neck became clammy with it; my hands juddered softly inside their respective pockets, and my breaths stuttered on their way in and out. I reached to a nearby railing to steady myself and tried to force my breathing into some regularity before I continued with the final few feet of the journey. But still– *Should breathing be this hard?* I wondered as I massaged the centre of my chest, as though there were something physical obstructing my airway – rather than it being clogged by ill feeling instead.

It was only late afternoon but the sky had dipped into

greyscale and charcoal already. It gave the station an even more foreboding look. Though it still couldn't compare with the appearance of the prison proper, which looked fit for a B-listed horror film. There was a flurry of activity stemming from a group of uniform officers who had stepped outside in a huddle. I waited at the edge of the car park while they climbed into their vehicles and disappeared in their many directions. I wondered whether they had reasons for leaving, or whether it was anticipatory; though I supposed these days, one very quickly turned into the other. The front of the station lulled to a quiet then and I trod the rest of the way between the car park's edge and the door, only to be halted in my tracks as the door banged open again. It knocked back into the brick wall behind it and I winced; there was a pane of glass in the top panel, and I wasn't sure it would survive the impact. I was ready to judge the door-opener for their carelessness when I realised it was actually Rule who'd been responsible. I watched as she ran a hand through her mane of hair. Rule's hand settled around the back of her neck, and with her free hand she reached into the back pocket of her perfectly creased grey trousers.

I hadn't realised she was a smoker. She and I had spent what I thought probably counted as a significant amount of time together now, and never once had there been even so much as a whisper of the smell on her. But there she was, arguing with a lighter against the winter breeze. But by the time I'd closed the distance between us there was a thin plume of smoke rising from the end of her cigarette. When she exhaled she looked like a dragon. I wondered whether that was a comparison her colleagues had made. It couldn't have been easy for her, being a hard-edged woman in a hard-edged man's world. The latter was a character people welcomed, expected even; whereas the former, in my experience, translated to something unwomanly and often unwelcome. I felt for her, in some ways.

'Maggie.' She smiled when she spotted me. 'I was told you were coming.' She swapped hands to hold her cigarette further away from me, then reached out for a shake with her other. 'Sorry, it's a disgusting habit but–'

'You've got a very stressful job,' I said, interrupting her.

She tilted her head to one side and cocked an eyebrow. 'Well, there is that.'

I shifted from one foot to the other. It was two parts cold; eight parts nerves. I thought of asking whether she'd mind if I went in ahead of her. Though that put me in the position of facing off against Kitsell and Thompson while we all waited for Rule to finish her cigarette break anyway, and I decided that I liked my chances more in this cold air than I did in the warm interior of the station.

'How are you doing?' she asked then.

I shrugged. 'I don't know how to answer that.'

'Which I can understand.' She took another deep draw of smoke into her mouth; it poured out in a torrent when she spoke again. 'Actually, I can't understand, of course. It's insensitive of me to imply that I can. I can't even– There's no way for me to imagine what it is you're going through.'

'Are you married?' The question erupted out of me like a hiccup. No sooner had it emerged and I was desperate to draw it back in. 'Sorry, that's personal, I shouldn't–'

'Please, don't apologise. No, I'm not married.' She paused for another inhale. 'I've got two daughters, though, about the same age as your sons, I'd wager. Diane and Patti. Patricia, really, but she hates it, says it's old-fashioned.'

'I think most children hate their names.'

'Otis and Finn are nice names, distinct.'

I was reminded, then, of how much this woman knew of me without my having told her, and the thought sent an itching through my skin.

'Finn is short for Finley. I don't know where it came from, really. Edward chose it.' *All roads lead back to him*, I thought then, though I tried to shake the thought away before it could take root. 'Otis was my choice.'

There was a long pause where it was all too apparent that neither of us knew what to say. While the space around us must have been busy, somehow the only clear sound I could hold on to was the burn of Rule's cigarette as she took one drag and then another in rapid succession. She leaned back against the wall of the station, one foot propped up behind her, and she looked every bit the archetypal tough police officer. It was almost laughable, the mimicry between her and the fictional detectives I had grown up watching on television.

'Kitsell thinks you're here to call the whole thing off.' She said it with such ease that I wondered whether, despite my concerns, my guilt, the plan to pull out of this mightn't be as unreasonable as I'd first thought it was. 'Is he right?'

'Yes.' I tried to match her ease but my voice shook all the same. 'I think he is.'

Rule dabbed her cigarette out on the wall, and I thought that was her way of signalling the conversation as one that needed to be moved inside. But instead she reached behind her to pull another one free of the packet.

'I have to applaud you getting this far.'

I stifled a laugh; I knew the sound would be sarcastic, hard. Rule didn't deserve that reaction when she was only trying to be kind to me as I faced off against something unfathomably unkind.

'I'm not sure I deserve much applause,' I answered.

'You've helped us find out a lot of information that we didn't have to begin with.'

'But it's not everything, is it?'

Rule seemed to hesitate before she responded. 'No, no, it's not everything.'

'Though I've wondered whether Edward ever really will tell me everything.'

'You doubt him?'

That time, I did laugh. But Rule took the reaction well and matched it with her own wide smile. 'Of course you doubt him. He's a serial murderer.' She inhaled again, punctuating the sentence with a crackle and burn. 'But then, he has been honest with us so far.'

'So far,' I echoed. 'But he still won't answer my questions about Lucy.'

'Can you live with not knowing?' she asked without missing a beat. I don't know what look I cut her but she threw one hand up as though in defence. 'I'm playing devil's advocate, obviously. If you can live with not knowing *and* if you've reached the limit on this, which incidentally, *none* of us would harbour bad feelings about, then you're welcome to go in there and prove to Kitsell what a good detective he still is.' She made it sound like a joking matter when of course, it was anything but. I appreciated the effort. 'Again, Maggie, I can't– It is beyond me, to understand how hard it is to be doing this.'

'You're going through it, too,' I answered, 'you're hearing all of the... things.'

'I have a vested interest.'

'Because of your job?'

'Because I have daughters.' She extinguished her second cigarette and dropped it into the ashtray that was fixed to the wall. 'I can't tidy up every corner of the world but I can sure as shit try to make a difference as I go. And I like to think that if I lost a daughter, and I never really knew what had happened to her, there'd be someone out there fighting my corner for answers, too...'

TWENTY

'You're trying to tell me you didn't do *anything* for your birthday?'

Edward had been pushing the same question intermittently since we arrived in the room that day. He would answer one or two of my queries and then match them with his own, which was always this. I couldn't decide whether it was nosiness that made him ask, or whether he only wanted me to know that he'd remembered. Because there had been one year when he hadn't. He'd told me that he had to take a trip for work over a weekend. My birthday fell on the Saturday, but I said nothing; he said nothing. Until he got home, that is, the penny having dropped sometime, midway between his lengthy drive out of one town and into a major city, between his drinks with insurance executives from his firm. Edward had been a salesman for years at that point; it was what he was good at, convincing people of what they needed, lying to them about how safe they were. It had been a good weekend, he'd said, but he would have rather been at home celebrating with me. Though the fact that he'd gone through three phone calls without so much as wishing me a happy birthday had been clue enough that the date had missed his mind. At the time, I was hurt. Now, I was curious.

'Do you remember the year you forgot my birthday entirely?'

He flinched. 'That was a mistake.'

'So, yes.' I smiled. 'Where were you again? Was it Leeds?'

Edward flashed his shark grin but somehow the threat of it had lessened. I had come to appreciate that if you were swimming in infested waters, you couldn't be surprised when a great white unhinged its mouth in front of you.

'Leeds, for work.'

'Didn't you go there more than once?'

'For work? I don't think so.'

'I wasn't asking for work.'

Edward huffed a laugh. 'You're getting better at asking your own questions, Maggie, but don't dance around it.' He leaned forward on the table and spoke in a near whisper. 'What are you really trying to ask?'

I pulled in a deep breath and exhaled the question. 'Did you murder a woman in—'

'Yes,' he snapped – and he looked pleased with himself when he said it.

The back of my throat began to sting with the rise of bile. I had tried to start eating more but it hadn't mattered; I would never be able to ingest enough food to counteract the amount of sickness that swilled out of me every day that I saw Edward – and even on some days when I didn't see him at all, but instead thought of him too much.

'What happened to Cinders?'

It was *such* an unexpected question that I thought it had knocked Edward with a physical force. He leaned back in his chair and pulled his forehead into folds of confusion. I imagined Kitsell and Rule wearing similar expressions in the adjoining room. Newell and Thompson were elsewhere, working on I-didn't-know-what, but I thought when they reviewed the tape later they would likely be surprised, too.

'The cat?'

'The cat.'

The boys had been desperate for a pet. Edward had steadfastly denied them that wish. It began with pleas for a dog which allowed Edward the easy rebuttal regarding the general upkeep of a dog, how much attention they require, how much walking; as though our kind and lively boys were opposed to attention and exercise. Then, it became a plea for a cat. Otis was the ringleader – Otis was always the ringleader – with a chalkboard presentation of bullet points detailing the many reasons why it was good and sensible for us to get a cat. He and Finn had asked to see Edward and I in the living room. They had sat us down on the two-seater and asked that we save any questions until the end. It had always been a happy memory; the moment when the boys broke their father's resolve.

Cinders was a black and ginger creature with a sour face and a soft nature. The boys had fallen in love with her, and even I had taken to her small invasions around my otherwise neat home: mice left on the doorstep; paw prints in the butter, if I left it uncovered for too long; hairballs behind the sofa. Some of her behaviours were more bearable than others – like all of us. That's what I'd told Edward when he regaled me again with tales of cat hair on the roof of his car from Cinders having slept there, small tears in a work shirt that she happened to have kneaded, the echoes of scratches down his forearms when he'd tried to wrestle her away from something she shouldn't have been doing. Needless to say, Edward and Cinders did not have an easy bond.

We only had her for eight months before she disappeared. It was the same day that Edward had his car valeted. I had always thought there existed connective tissue between those two things. But asking outright had once terrified me.

'What happened to Cinders?' I repeated when he didn't answer.

'She just went missing, didn't she?'

'No, we told the boys she went missing.'

'What's the difference?' He laughed, but instead of it being his typical cocksure sound, there was something nervous in the noise instead.

'Did you hit her with the car on purpose?'

Even after all this, I was still giving him some benefit of the doubt.

He sighed and dropped his hands into his lap. It was the first confession he'd made when he hadn't been able to look me in the eye as he said it. 'Yes, I hit her on purpose.'

I felt relief – no, not relief, vindication. 'And?'

'And she's buried in the back garden of our old house.'

'I'll let the boys know.'

'Do you think they'll care?' He sounded spiteful. When he looked up at me his face was pulled tight, his mouth wrinkled around the question. 'It's been a long time, Maggie, I'm sure they've long forgotten about what happened.'

'If that sentiment were in any way true then we wouldn't be in this room.'

Edward, somehow, seemed to have regained his footing as we edged around the topic of Cinders. His expression loosened, his mouth slackened into a smile, and again he asked, 'So are you going to tell me what you did for your birthday?'

'Do you know the name of the woman in Leeds?'

From his expression it was easy enough to learn his answer. To him, she would have been the same as the others: anonymous.

'I'll be seeing you,' I said as I stood from the table then. It was usually Edward's line but there was a slight satisfaction to be gained in hearing it said in my own voice. 'It'll be a couple of days before I'm back, if not longer.'

'Call first,' he said, 'I might have plans.'

Unless the plans are suicide or sudden demise then I couldn't care. The thought startled me, but I realised, too, that I really did mean it.

I waited for the lock of the door to click and release me. When I tumbled from one room into the other I found that I was gasping for air; a fish, freed from infested waters. Rule brought a can of Coca-Cola across to me – 'The sugar will help.' – and cupped the ball of my shoulder. She guided me towards the centre table, where Kitsell was waiting with a chair pulled out for me.

'You showed a lot of balls in there today.' Rule sounded impressed. 'We'll pass everything along to Thompson and Newell, and they'll get to work liaising with cold-case teams up north to see if there's anything in the Leeds area that we can trace.'

'I can't believe that fucker killed a cat,' Kitsell said, more to himself, as though that were the final straw in this whole mess. 'Will you actually tell the boys?'

I shook my head. 'They don't need that hurt.' I turned and looked through the window into the interview room. Edward was still sitting there, waiting for his guide, guard, to lead him from the room. 'I'm not going back in there,' I clarified.

'No, no, you absolutely aren't,' Rule reassured me. She squatted so we were face to face as she spoke. 'They can come and fetch him whenever they're ready. I'm only interested in you at the minute.'

'I'm fine, really. The sugar will help, like you said.' I took another sip from the drink. It was all syrup and, even though I knew it was a psychosomatic response, my teeth ached under the grit of it. 'Speaking to him, knowing what he did, what he was doing, it's all a shock still, isn't it? But I think I'm improving. Don't you both think I'm improving?' I looked from Rule to Kitsell, who I had to crane my neck to see properly. His face was set with anger and I could see that he was still staring into Edward, and likely hadn't heard my question.

'There's something else we need to talk to you about, Maggie,' Rule said then. Her face was adorned with a thin smile, and I thought she looked nervous.

'Are the boys okay?' I snapped. They were always my closest worry.

'The boys are fine.' Kitsell broke his stare then and came to stand behind Rule, who was still crouched level with my seat. 'The boys are absolutely fine. But there's a chance we may not be able to keep the boys out of this for much longer.'

'I...' I shook my head. 'I don't think I understand.'

'Maggie,' Rule couldn't look at me, 'there's been a leak.'

It is testimony to how far removed I was from their world, from this world, that my immediate response was, 'At the house?' But when Rule gave me a pitying look I understood the error of the question. My shoulders dropped under the weight of having realised. 'No, of course not at the house.'

'It's important that we count our blessings here, because so far they don't seem to know your name,' Kitsell rushed to reassure me. 'They're talking about O'Connor's wife, and they've only printed your old name.'

Of course, when Kitsell said my old name he meant my real name; the name I had shaken my arms free of and dropped to the floor like an outdated jacket. I had been so many people since being Edward O'Connor's wife.

My worry jerked forwards again. 'The boys?'

'The boys haven't been mentioned at all. So far, all they seem to know is that you're helping us, and that Edward has made a number of confessions that we're resultantly investigating,' she parroted what I imagined they'd printed, 'but we are going to have to be careful from here on.'

'Careful how?'

Rule righted herself and stood along Kitsell. It was him that answered, after an uncomfortable quiet had elbowed against the walls. 'We've booked you into a hotel. If you let us know the things you'd like from home, we can get those for you. But on the off-chance that someone does work out who you are, now, we need to make sure you're protected.'

'So help me, God, Maggie.' Rule ran a hand through her hair how she had done outside the station. There was a creep of red appearing from behind the top of her roll-neck jumper. 'I'm going to find out where this leak is and I'm going to have it suspended.'

I tried to smile like I believed her. But the expression felt weak. I thought of the boys again then, and I wondered whether I should have changed their names when I had the chance. *Thank God, they haven't been printed*, I thought over and again while Kitsell helped me from my seat, Rule held the door open, the guards said their sad farewells to me for the day, knowing what had happened, *thank God, the boys haven't been printed*. There wasn't much else that I cared about in the world in those moments apart from them. Certainly not Edward; certainly not myself. The press could have my name if that's what they were hungry for. I even began to wonder – while sitting in the back seat of a blacked-out vehicle, on the way to a hotel I didn't know the name of – whether it mightn't bring with it a sort of relief.

TWENTY-ONE

It was generic but not inexpensive. Though I didn't know where the hotel was exactly, in relation to my own home, I did know that it took Kitsell thirty-five minutes to drive there. I couldn't be outside of the town limits, I guessed, but my new postcode was hidden on the fringes. I assumed that they thought it was a safe distance – either that, or a convenient one. It had been two days since they'd brought me here. In that time I had slept little, eaten less, and asked Rule for a cigarette on two separate occasions.

'I didn't realise you smoked.'

'I don't,' I answered, my hand outstretched in readiness for her lighter.

Edward and I had both moved through a period of smoking, somewhere in our late teens and into our very early twenties. It was a blissful time when no one knew what smoking did to you; we only knew how it made us feel. With a cigarette hanging out from between reddened lips and my boyfriend's arm tucked around me, both of us wearing leather blazers and badges, I had felt like a poster child for something, somewhere, much bigger and cooler than the space in which I actually resided: a middle-class estate in a far corner of the West Midlands, where my mother would tell me to wipe my mouth clean when I walked through the door. It wasn't quite the same, Rule and I lingering in the smoking area of the hotel bar to avoid being seen out front, neither of us feeling particularly cool unless we were talking in reference to the weather, which seemed to have dropped into deep winter overnight. I wondered whether it was pathetic fallacy.

'Is there anything else you need from your home?'

Rule had already invaded that space – with my permission, but it had been an invasion nevertheless. I told her to choose from the clothes as it suited her and she'd returned with my best and favourite knitwear, as though she could sense my preference for it based on the wool balls that had formed through years of wear. She brought jeans and pumps and only one set of pyjamas. To begin with I thought this was a sign that I mightn't stay here for long, that it might all be over soon. Now, I was under no such illusion. She had asked, twice now, whether there was anything else I needed. It wasn't that I would be freed soon; it was only that Rule didn't mind making multiple trips for anything left behind. I considered asking for my key back.

'I have everything for now, thank you,' I said instead and then I threw my cigarette into an ashtray on a nearby table. It extinguished with a hiss as it hit the rainwater in the shallow bowl. 'I'm going to go back to the room and get some more work done.'

It was a lie. I hadn't managed to work in two days.

'Maggie, you should really try to eat something.'

Rule had noticed that I was living predominantly on black coffee. Nothing was sacred or hidden when your only company was a team of revolving detectives.

'Why don't I order something for us both, have it sent up to the room?'

I scrunched up my face. 'Honestly, I'm fine.'

'Do you have a preference for anything, or anything you hate?' she asked as though I hadn't spoken at all. 'Because without some guidance I'm just going to get a heinous selection of things and charge all of it to the room.' She reached out to squeeze my forearm. 'There have to be some perks to the situation.'

I managed a smile. 'In which case, I think I'd prefer a bottle of wine.' I wasn't being serious – but if wine arrived outside my door, I decided it wouldn't be the worst thing either.

'I'll have another one of these,' she fumbled to free the cigarettes from her pocket, 'and then I'll browse the menu.'

'Thank you.'

I ducked into the hotel bar and weaved my way through the patrons without making eye contact. Kitsell and Thompson had assured me I was safe, but despite that I much preferred to keep my face hidden for the time being – even if it was a face marked by age and stress and worry, and markedly different to the face that journalists had last hungrily taken photographs of, on the ways in and out of court hearings. Once I was stashed away inside the lift I braved a look at myself then, in the mirrored wall at the back of the space. Typically, I thought I appeared tired. Now, I was whatever comes beyond it. There were cushions of exhaustion beneath each eye and a purple tinge to my cheeks. I would need to wear make-up the next time I saw Edward. *I will need Rule to fetch make-up for me before the next time I see Edward,* I corrected as I lowered my gaze and turned to face the lift doors instead. Apparently it wasn't only strangers and journalists I couldn't bear to look in the eye – but myself now, too.

A tidal wave of relief washed over me when I stepped into the room again. The temperature wasn't right, the wall hangings were hideous, and I was perturbed by an adjoining bathroom that *only* had a bath with no shower fitment to speak of. For now, though, this was home. I slipped off my shoes by the door and crossed the space to the bed, where my laptop was already waiting. I eyed the tea and coffee facilities for a second but cautioned myself against it; if Rule had taken me seriously about the suggestion of wine, I would wait for that. Though it was usually an activity that I savoured with the jumping bean anxiety caused by my caffeine intake and strength, I backed up against my plush pillows and opened my laptop. After I typed in my password – one of the few remnants of privacy left – the webpage unfolded onto an estate agent's website. The house was one hundred and thirty-six miles away. I thought the boys would understand.

The information was so outdated – or rather, not outdated, but recycled. Each news story became a rehash of an older one, with creative flare added sparingly throughout for colour, for human interest. The most striking editorial decision of them all was when one newspaper opted to make Lucy into a cover girl; her face the centred display on both website and print versions of the publication. When I clicked into the webpage her smile appeared in slow and jagged movements, and while everything in me wanted to close the window, I found somehow that I couldn't bring myself to look away either. The story was one designed to tug on the heartstrings, relaying what a promising young woman she had been, how missed she was by everyone around her. The writer had tried hard to create pathos between their piece and a reader but, I thought, it was all too much effort; the writer had tried much too hard. They hadn't needed to remind a reader of how promising a young woman Lucy had been; they *all* were. If they hadn't been, people wouldn't still be interested in them.

'That's a harsh perspective,' Kitsell said from the corner of the room. He was sitting in an armchair with his feet propped up on the window ledge, a copy of the paper spread wide and gaping between his hands. His positioning made Lucy's view of me inescapable, long after I'd closed the webpage even. 'I don't think it's their youth and promise that makes them memorable.'

'What is it then?' I asked as I clicked from one online paper to the next.

'The fact that they were murdered.'

I glanced up at him from behind the screen, in anticipation of a greater reasoning than that. But he only shrugged, ruffling the paper in the process. I shook my head then, and shifted my stare back to the screen. 'People don't remember the names of murdered women just because they were murdered women.'

'Maggie, this room is making you–'

'How many serial murderers can you name?' I said, interrupting him.

He looked out of the window and exhaled hard. 'I honestly don't know.'

'How many of their victims can you name?'

Kitsell managed something like a chuckle before he answered. 'I honestly don't know.'

'I see.' I nodded and narrowed my eyes. 'For the same reason? Or because you can remember *so* many of one and so few of the other?'

'Why don't you go back to looking for your name in the headlines?'

'You make it sound narcissistic,' I snapped, 'I want to know whether they know me.'

'They don't.' Something in Kitsell's tone had changed then; he'd moved from sarcasm through to sadness. 'They know who you used to be when you were married to Edward. That's all they know, Maggie.'

'They seem to know he's confessed to new crimes.'

I skimmed the news story attached to the headline 'O'Connor Kills in Retrospect: How many more to come?'. Still, there was no mention of me or my involvement. There was only reference to "a source" and "someone close to O'Connor". *In proximity alone,* I thought with a measure of spite. There was nothing about the boys in this story either, which at least afforded me some relief. Any mention of them – not here specifically, but in the reports across the many publications I'd swallowed in recent days – had only been vague and uncertain remarks: "The area where O'Connor had lived with his wife and two children..." or "O'Connor will be survived by his ex-wife and two children..." from one reporter who was clearly so eager for Edward to die that they were writing his obituary in advance. It became one of two thoughts that brought me comfort during the days sequestered in that hotel room: the boys were safe, and one day Edward will die.

'Christ, it's cold out there.' Rule burst into the room and rubbed her reddened hands together, with so much enthusiasm that the gesture looked cartoonish. Before I knew she was a smoker, I'd never once sniffed it on her. Since finding out, it was all I could smell when she walked into a room. It was better than perfume, I had decided, but not as good as smoking first-hand, which I was desperately trying not to do. 'Everyone okay in here?'

'Rule,' Kitsell lowered his paper, 'how many victims of serial murder can you name?'

She shrugged. 'Fewer than the killers I can name, I'd guess. Why?'

Kitsell looked at me and shook his head, as though outraged that my cynicism held some truth.

'Kitsell and I were just talking about the social culture of serial murder.'

Rule squinted at me. 'You need to read something that isn't a newspaper.'

'I'm looking for the boys.'

'We're looking for the boys.' She pointed to Kitsell and his growing pile of periodicals. 'We're watching the media, Maggie, I can promise you. If there's a mention of your name, or the boys' names, we'll be all over the author like you can't believe. Until then–'

'Sit tight and appear when summoned?'

'That isn't what I was going to say, at all.' She landed hard on the bed and reached over to close my laptop. I didn't like the gesture, and if I'd been doing work then I would have liked it even less. It was one of many demonstrations of Rule and her assumed command of people's attentions; there had been a lot of that in recent days. 'What will help you?'

'I want to see my children.'

She looked at Kitsell as she answered. 'Okay.'

There was a ruffle from the corner of the room; I could hear Kitsell's disapproval in the way he collapsed the newspaper into an accordion of stories. Rule had evidently been waiting for that reaction, too, her eyebrow already raised and a smirk in place that seemed to denote her readiness for an argument.

'Maggie, if you want to see your children, then see your children,' she turned to face me then, 'you're aware of what the risks are, but you're also an adult and not under arrest.'

'I'm not going to disappear into the night,' I reassured her, already tugging my phone free of my front pocket, 'I only want to see they're okay. These stories can't be pleasant for them either.'

The boys had been lucky, I thought, to have only been mentioned in passing, anonymously, as though they had been struck from the record of Edward's misdemeanours. For a time both of them had changed their names as frequently as I changed mine, with every house move, school change, career swap. But the closer they reached to adulthood the more defiant they both became, and instead of abandoning their birth names entirely they had only abandoned the family one. They had re-emerged as their old selves – Otis and Finn as we'd christened them – though neither of them held on to O'Connor, instead adopting two different and distinct surnames to each other; brothers in blood alone. So the breadcrumb trail leading to their identities may have been smudged along the forest floor over the intervening years. But I still had my worries about their names being revealed – and deeper, hidden worries, about why they hadn't been already...

TWENTY-TWO

Edward had always had the most beautiful hazel eyes I had ever seen. As a teenager I'd always imagined the man of my dreams to have blue eyes – and most likely blond hair, owing to urban myths about this being the perfect combination of colours. But when Edward had stared deep into my eyes at the end of our first evening together, even as a teenager I had known in the bowl of my nervous stomach that they were eyes I could happily look into for a long time – no matter their colour.

A long time had ended, and that afternoon Edward looked at me with eyes that appeared drained of their colour entirely. I had heard eyes described as grey before though I'd never been able to pair the description with the object. Now, as he stared hard at me through narrowed slits, the only colour I could discern was too light to be blue; nowhere near dark enough to denote hazel. Edward looked as though someone had put his appearance through a photo-app editor, turning colours up and down until what remained was closer to pop-culture artwork rather than an accurate rendering of the man himself. His skin, no longer as pale as it had been, had yellowed since my last visit; his hair somehow looked darker, or maybe it only seemed it in contrast to his complexion; and his fingers, tapping rhythmically against the table, looked elongated, flesh loosely wrapped around bone.

Twenty minutes had passed in this room with both of us saying little to the other. It was apparent to anyone watching that we had brought our respective baggage with us today, and it made idle conversation feel impossible.

'I'll tell you what's up with me if you tell me what's up with you.'

The offer came as such as surprise that I flinched. My head jerked backwards in answer.

'You're my wife,' Edward continued, his tapping ceased, 'is it so strange to think I'd want to know if something were wrong with you?'

'Ex-wife,' I corrected, 'and you never wanted to know when something was wrong when we were married so–'

'So give a dying man his final wish.'

My jaw tightened. 'I already am.'

Edward laughed and snapped his fingers. 'Quick, Maggie, quick. Be careful you don't cut yourself on that tongue.' He awkwardly folded his arms and leaned towards me. 'So am I telling you what's wrong with me or not?'

'I'm not striking a quid pro quo with you.'

'Okay, well I don't know what that means exactly so I'll tell you anyway, and if you decide you want to tell me your stuff after then you can go ahead. How does that sound?' He didn't wait for an answer, per se, only made an additional awkward effort to try to crack his knuckles all together – I winced at the sound, nervous that the applied pressure might cause a break – before launching into his own tirade. 'I am choosing to die, right? I am making that choice. But as of yesterday, I can't get pain relief. I can't get any bloody relief from this,' he shifted to point at his side; I wasn't sure which organ it was meant to denote, 'or this,' he said, pointing to another area in his abdomen. 'I can't get relief from any of it, because we're staring down the barrel of six months, and this is when it starts to get worse, they tell me. This is when shit gets real.'

I would have thought shit got real when Edward was diagnosed with cancer, but apparently suffering a physical ill in accompaniment to that cancer was a stride too far. I didn't know what he'd expected though; whether he'd thought the disease might take him quietly if he didn't put up a fight.

'You refused treatment.'

He held up a finger as though to underscore the incoming point. 'But that doesn't mean refusing drugs.'

'For Christ's sake, Edward, you *refused* treatment. Your cancer escalated, has escalated, as they said it would. You're the mastermind behind a double-figure bloody murder spree, don't try to tell me you're stupid enough to have thought dying from cancer wouldn't be a touch uncomfortable for you.'

Edward placed one hand flat on his chest and tried to mime wiping a tear away with the other. 'Honestly, Maggie, when you're soft with me like this, I just– I never know how– It's almost too much for my failing heart.'

'If only it were that easy.'

'Maggie, I'm telling you I've got six months left.'

'And I'm asking you if that's how long this will take?'

Edward dropped back in his seat. His hands were clasped together on the table in front of him, and he stared searchingly into his palms. 'Jesus, Maggie, if you hadn't just called me a mastermind then I'd be starting to doubt whether you care about me at all, the way you're speaking to me today.'

I slammed my hands so hard on the table that he flinched, and I enjoyed seeing that surprise in him. I stood, leaving both hands in place, and when I was upright I gave the table an abrupt shove. It didn't move an inch, owing to being bolted to the floor, but I had to hope the gesture still carried some weight.

'I am fucking done.'

'Maggie!'

I was only two steps towards the door when he shouted after me. I imagined Rule, Newell and Kitsell in the adjoining room, running their hands through their hair, their eyes wide and their mouths dry with panic. Thompson, I thought, was likely smirking – or perhaps even cheering me on.

'Jesus, don't storm out. What the hell has happened? Are the kids okay?'

I laughed; a sharp huff of a sound that caught at the back of my throat. He knew me well enough, still, to know that if something were wrong then the most likely root cause would be the boys. Though I would have bet money that even Edward couldn't make a more specific guess at what had happened to render my mood quite so brittle.

'You've been made aware that you're back in the papers?'

He held his hands up in a defensive gesture. 'They already spoke to me about that.'

And Rule had. Edward had been the first piece of deadwood they'd checked for signs of a leak. He had, as promised, told his prying prison family that he was talking to the police about crimes he hadn't disclosed details of the first time around; he allegedly hadn't been more specific than that, and Rule nor Thompson had been able to disprove the claim. Regrettably, no one had thought to check my own vessel for signs of wood rot. While everyone had been looking in the wrong directions, there had been a mutiny aboard my own rocking ship...

'*Otis* told the papers?'

There was a strangled cry caught in the chamber of my throat. I only nodded and then swallowed hard, afraid that if I tried to form a verbal answer an animal wail might come out. I wondered whether this revenge tragedy – this punishment of the mother by the child – was something that even existed in the animal world, or whether it was another thing afforded to we humans in exchange for opposable thumbs and voice-activation technology. Given the pain that was swelling in my stomach like a third offspring, I would have happily given up both thumbs and my access to Siri, if someone could only un-strand the tapestry weave my son had formed from falsities and facts, pitched to the highest bidder. Though – the saving grace, perhaps – at least it hadn't been for actual money.

'What the hell was it for then?'

Unable to stand under the weight of Edward's questions any longer, I trod back to my seat. I landed hard, pressed my elbows on the table's edge, and held my head in my palms. 'I think he did it to punish me, for this.' When I chanced a look upward I saw Edward's face had pulled together in an observable confusion. He looked as though someone had presented him with an equation relating to string theory. 'He spoke to a reporter after my birthday, by all accounts,' I carried on, as though *more* information would make the first reveal easier to digest, though I knew from experience that wasn't the case. The more Otis had explained it all to me – unashamedly, might I add – the less understanding I had of what might drive someone's own child to strike at them with quite such a sting. 'It looks to have been a reporter who actually has some morals, so at least Otis was fortunate in that respect. The woman he spoke to, she works with *The Local Star*, she agreed to keep his and Finn's names out of it, whatever happens.'

'Like other newspapers won't just go ahead and print their names anyway?'

I shrugged. 'They haven't so far.'

'It's a matter of time.'

'Maybe so. But he struck a deal for it, and it seems to have worked for him.'

'So what, he gave them information in exchange for keeping their names…' Edward petered out when he spotted the slow shake of my head. 'Bastard,' he whispered but no sound was sacred inside this shell of a room and somehow the noise seemed to echo. My eyes snapped wide in answer. 'He gave them *you*.'

'Yes and no. They don't know my name, as it is now.'

'Like they won't go ahead and find–'

'They haven't so far,' I parroted.

'Jesus, if I could get my hands on the kid.' He pushed hard against the table as though trying to tip back on his chair. Both were bolted to the floor, albeit with aged screws, so their movement was limited – and Edward's strength wasn't what it used to be. That much was evident from the frown that accompanied his force, and the flicker of pain that followed, too. 'Does Finn know?'

'I didn't think to ask.'

Otis had been so quick to admit what he'd done that I'd wondered since whether he'd admitted it with a savage sense of pride, too. When Rule had told me I could see the boys, I hadn't even thought to call ahead. It was the first time I'd arrived at Otis's home unannounced, and it had been by chance that I'd gone to him first; the hotel, I had learned, was closer to his home than it was to Finn's. There was a real possibility that, had I gone the extra proverbial mile and landed on Finn's doorstep instead, I mightn't have found out what Otis had done. Emilia had ushered me out of the cold and welcomed me into their home, though it was clear that both her and Otis hadn't long returned from their days at their respective offices. Emilia apologised for the state she was in – her words – and disappeared for a shower, though she welcomed me to stay for dinner before she left. Meanwhile, Otis had only greeted me with a set expression, his arms folded and his demeanour rich with having hard-talked with colleagues for the day; he brought his tone into our conversation, too, when Emilia was out of earshot and he asked me plainly what I was doing visiting without having asked. I hadn't even had time to answer when he threw another question into the stale air between us.

'Oh,' he'd said, 'you know?'

And then somehow, without him even having told me, yes, I knew.

'He needs to learn some fucking respect, never mind anything else.'

'And you'll be the person to teach him that, will you?' My tone was flat, deadpan, and Edward looked wounded by it. 'What do you plan on doing exactly, writing him a strongly worded letter care of His Majesty's Prison Service?'

Edward forced out a long breath and I couldn't decide whether he was breathing through rage or pain. There was the same map of a frown on his forehead. It was a violent and unexpected intrusion for me to remember him then as he had been twenty-something years ago, leaning over the tap in the bathroom with a precursor to this frown, the lines not quite as deep or pronounced, age not yet having overtaken his face. Though our life together was peppered with unpleasant memories, this filtered back in as a moment of fondness, a moment of care where I had said something was wrong and Edward had said–

'Let me help.'

It took me a moment to realise he'd spoken in the now, not the then.

'Seriously, Maggie, what can I– There must be something I can be doing?'

Rule had sent me in here with a clear instruction: names and places. There were two slips of paper folded over each other in the back pocket of my trousers, with a small betting-shop pencil. I freed them both then and placed them on the table between us.

'Give me something I can give to them.'

Edward acquiesced, but he did so begrudgingly. He took the pencil and awkwardly started to write down names. He was inhibited by the handcuffs and, I soon realised, a physical difficulty in gripping the pencil. I took the materials back then but urged him to continue, and I hurriedly annotated both sheets with spots around the country where my husband may or may not have attacked women; where he may or may not have killed them.

TWENTY-THREE

After learning of Otis's betrayal, after playing secretary to Edward in his documentation of crimes, there was a feeling in me that I thought could only be described as a loss. I wandered around in the days that followed with my shoulders slumped and my mouth thickly coated with caffeine and nicotine, and I felt a deep-rooted grief that sat in my sternum with roots that stretched deep into my bowels and pelvis. It was a consuming feeling, the whole world tinged in this off-white where nothing was wrong exactly, but nothing looked how it had done either. I thought I could remember this sensation from before – before the police, before the courts, before I knew – and I harboured ill feeling to my husband and son alike for causing a second wave of it. I could believe it of Edward, but Otis, Otis was where the real Shakespearean tragedy lay.

I shared the slips of paper with Rule after I left Edward, and I rebuffed the sympathies of her and Kitsell for Otis having given us all up to the papers. They were gentle, tender with me. I was more thankful to Thompson, for his hard clamp on the shoulder, his tut and his eye-roll as though to say, 'Kids, eh?' It crossed my mind that I should apologise to them all, not only for blowing the quiet of their operation – after I had begged them so determinedly for it in the first instance – but also for the time they had spent looking for the leak within their own department. Over and again I drafted apologies that my mouth couldn't form; I was so tired of apologising for one of the men in my life, I realised that I simply did not have the energy to begin again, apologising for another.

The information gave them a lot to be getting along with and, in exchange for it, I begged their quiet. Thompson agreed to that much, whether Kitsell or Rule required anything more from me or not. He decided to take me back to the hotel, where he ordered me a plain pizza and a large bottle of white wine without asking, while I was outside inhaling the last cigarette I had promised myself I wouldn't smoke. Thompson had stocked me up with another packet of cigarettes and an additional two bottles of wine before he'd left that night.

'I don't know what your poison is,' he'd said as he handed over the goods, 'but I thought you deserved something. Food, booze and smokes must cover that something.' I had laughed then, albeit a faint and tired sound. 'If you need anything, call me.' He turned to head for the door of the hotel room but then changed direction. 'Unless you want sympathy, then–'

'Call Kitsell,' I'd interrupted him.

He'd snapped his fingers. 'I knew you'd know.'

Sympathy sat on the fringes of my mind in the in-between days though. I was only ever at the hotel, never venturing out further than the beer garden for a cigarette beneath their heated canopy. If Rebecca called – which she did, twice – I told her only that I wasn't home and was unlikely to be any time soon. I didn't mind how vague it sounded, and I didn't feel like I owed her an explanation either, such was my disconnect by then. I missed three of my usual evenings at the food bank; I stopped thinking about the boys; I no longer browsed house listings on the internet. *And this,* I thought on day three of my self-imposed isolation, *is what it feels like to disappear.*

I was two clicks away from checking newspaper headlines – as though Otis deserved that concern from me still – when my phone hummed from somewhere in the bed. It had been swallowed by the duvet sometime during the night, but I eventually freed it from the foot of the bed in time to catch a call from–

'A number I don't recognise,' I said aloud while my thumb flirted with the answer button. I accepted the call but only held the phone to my ear, without offering my own greeting. There was a bustle in the background, an office maybe, and then a confused 'Hello?' from a voice that I recognised.

'DS Newell?'

'Hi, Maggie, yes, it's me.'

It was the first direct contact we'd had in what felt like a considerable time. Though time had now slipped into that strange loop where it both accelerates and slows, and all I could really say with any certainty was that Newell hadn't been at my last visit with Edward. I couldn't place whether he'd been at the visit before that one. I shook the detail away as inconsequential, though, and tried to focus on hearing his voice over the din of noise rising behind him.

'I'm sorry, it's difficult to catch what you're–'

'Let me move a second, Maggie, hang on.'

There came the distinct sensation of having been scooped up and physically moved, as though Newell had cupped my entire self in the bowl of his palm. He carried me into a quiet area and I heard the click of a door in the background as he sealed himself in.

'Sorry, there's a lot going on. I hope this is better?'

'What's going on?'

I didn't quite know how to handle Newell, owing to so many

of my interactions having been limited to Rule and, more often than not, Kitsell, too, as though he hadn't yet managed to move a safe distance away from the case and observe its newness as it unfolded. So I didn't know whether Newell responded well to bluntness, or whether my bluntness would lose me an ally in this mess. Either way, it was bad form to have dangled a carrot and then to expect the quality of our phone call connection to be the thing I cared about.

'The list of places that Edward gave us, you said you recognised some of them?'

My mouth was wrung dry of saliva and I thought my hard swallow might choke me. But then, a part of me might have been welcoming that. 'They were holiday destinations,' I managed another swallow, 'me and the boys, or sometimes Edward and I alone. Is there– Have you found...'

I didn't know what I was trying to ask so I let the sentence die quietly on the line.

'There are some pictures we'd like you to look at.' A long silence stretched between us where Newell's breathing escalated to hurried and my own slowed to a dangerous degree. 'Would that be okay, Maggie?' he asked after so long.

Do I have a choice? I wanted to ask, but Newell and I didn't know each other well enough for that yet. So I only agreed, and asked what time I should expect a car. Then I asked whether it was possible for Thompson to collect me. Then I asked whether he could bring cigarettes...

The girl was beautiful. Her smile was wide and orthodontist perfect; I looked for the echo of braces or another corrective fitment but I couldn't see anything to denote it. She wore minimal make-up, or else, she wore make-up that was well-disguised as minimal: a pale concealer, mascara that made her eyes wide and doe-like, a lick of lip balm that left a shine on her picture-perfect grin. The girl's hair was blonde, and it looked natural. There were no signs of brown or black roots along the parting, even though it also happened to be the same shade of blonde I was convinced did not exist on anyone above the age of three. It must have been summer when the picture was taken. She was wearing a white strap-top with a floral lace design that edged the top and bottom of the clothing; she'd paired it with denim shorts that had either been jeans in a former life, or they'd been ripped and stitched only to look as though they'd been rescued from a pair of jeans, it was impossible to tell which. The shorts weren't so short that, had I been her mother, I would have hailed her back in the house and demanded a change; though they were short enough to show young legs shaped by weekend sports and excellence awards at school. She was tanned, and that looked natural, too. There was nothing at all familiar about her – but there was no mistaking the fact that she was a girl.

'How old is she?'

'She was fifteen when that picture was taken,' Newell answered without looking at me – and I wondered whether he couldn't from empathy, or sympathy, or whether he couldn't because of what my husband might have done to this girl. A choked sound fell out of me when he confirmed her age, though, and I felt the ground tremor with something. 'She's the youngest victim we've found so far.'

'Victim of?'

'She was strangled,' Rule answered from behind me and the intrusion of her made me jump. My shoulders were still bunched uncomfortably when she came to a stop next to me and stared down at the map of photographs. They were pairing places with missing women. *Girls*, I corrected myself and a shudder moved through me at the thought.

'Was there anything– When she was taken, did anyone–' Each attempt was rebuffed by the sensation of bile rising through my body. I worried that I wouldn't get my sentences out ahead of any upchuck – or whether the two things were somehow part of the same guttural expulsion.

'There wasn't any interference with the body.' Rule had answered the question that I hadn't been brave enough to ask. And I physically doubled over with relief, using the table to support myself, my palms flat against it until I realised that meant I was leaning into the pictures of known and unknown victims of murder and assault. I snatched my hands back then, like a child caught against a hot stove, and I muttered my apologies to Rule who only waved them away how someone else might bat away a fly.

'Can you take Maggie through the rest of these images?' Rule asked her colleague from across the table. Newell scowled at her in answer, and it felt as though something passed between them. 'I need to make some calls,' she added in explanation. Rule set a hand on my shoulder then. 'We're not expecting miracles, but at this stage any information would be greatly appreciated.' She went to move away from the display but turned back to add, 'That stands for when you're talking to Edward next, too. All of this is at your disposal when it comes to rattling him, shaking anything loose...' She shrugged and I thought there might be more to the sentence, but instead she trod back in the direction of, I assumed, her office, leaving me with Newell and his display of dead girls.

'Don't mind her,' he said, as he began to rearrange stills for me to inspect, 'she's under a lot of pressure at the moment. We all are.' He huffed out a harsh noise and looked up at me. 'I didn't mean to imply by that that you aren't, obviously.'

Though Newell was likely older than both of my boys, there was something vulnerable about him in that moment that made me want to mother him. I reassured him that no offence was taken, before I probed into his superior's stern demeanour. It was something I was becoming accustomed to now, asking questions, the answers of which would likely scare me.

'She's stressed about Edward, or...?'

'Or.' Newell managed a smile. He rubbed at the back of his neck as he stood upright; I could see physical tension ebb away from him as he kneaded his muscles. 'The more we find out, Maggie...' His arm dropped heavily back down to his side. There was a hesitancy about him that helped to form a knot in my stomach; or a series of knots, like the balls of wool that my mother once gave me to untangle as a child. 'The more we find out, the more it looks as though we're staring down at one of the most prolific serial killers in British history. It's career-making stuff,' he said with what I thought was some satisfaction, 'but it's enough to break a person, too.'

TWENTY-FOUR

Though it felt dramatic to suggest it, life itself had become a source of exhaustion. Before Edward (the Return of), I had thought life was tiring because it was too empty. I held my routine of working, attending the food banks, socialising occasionally with Rebecca, forcing my children to socialise with me occasionally, too. It had crossed my mind that I was so tired all the time because there simply wasn't enough – but "not enough" was, I had always reasoned, precisely what I deserved, owing to my years of harbouring a villain, albeit unknowingly. Now, I reasoned that life was tiring because it was simply too much. I was working as best as I could given the circumstances; though my days now started with to-do lists formed of newspaper names and webzines that I needed to check, only to then be followed by the to-do lists for work. I had managed two phone calls with Rebecca where I had lied and told her only that I was busy with assignments, but I wanted to hear about her life and her daughters and her Zumba classes; I knew my fatigue had swooped to a new base level when I agreed to attend a class with her, too, 'once this was all out of the way', which she took to be a reference to work. I had even managed a handful of messages to Finn, who texted me with such apparent ease – asking after my well-being, and even asking after his father – that I realised he knew nothing of his brother's disloyalty. But these small and insignificant acts rendered me so tired, too tired, that when my hotel door was knocked against by Kitsell and Thompson or, very occasionally now, Rule, I found I had to unleash a small animal noise of exhaustion before I could even bring myself to attend to the visitor.

They never brought good news with them, and they never brought signs of an end. It had crossed my mind on more than one occasion that Edward's drip-feed of confessions would extend to the days when he was literally on his deathbed, and that thought exhausted me all the more. During some meetings he was so forthcoming with information that I could hardly stand it, and I left the room feeling physically wounded by the new leads he had bunched together for me – or rather, for the listening detectives. Then there were others where he was so vague, so keen, it seemed, to talk about everything *but* what he'd done, that I left with a different type of tiredness altogether; a tiredness tinged with sadness, that even the happiest of times in our lives was smoke-marked now by the reveals of his infidelities – for want of a better expression. I didn't know what else to call them.

I was, I thought, nearing a point where I would have to excuse myself from it all. I believed in penance but this winding road of it felt biblical, and I wasn't sure I had enough energy left in my tired bones to face over and again what felt very much like an Old Testament God.

'I don't know why you think you need penance in this situation at all,' Thompson answered me once, when I confided these feelings on a car journey to the prison. 'You never did anything wrong, Maggie. Believing your spouse, trusting him, that in itself isn't a crime. Or if it is, then it's one the majority of people are guilty of.' He spat out a harsh laugh. 'In fact, most people think it's an indiscretion if you *don't* trust your spouse. You ever think of it that way?' He side-eyed me as he drove and waited for an answer.

'No,' I said plainly as we pulled into a parking space near the entrance. I pulled my hood up and tightened it around my face, to shield myself from any overhead cameras or resourceful members of the press. 'No, I never think of it that way at all.'

When we stepped into our room that looked into the interview suite, Newell and Kitsell were already waiting. Neither of them said anything, but Kitsell's expression spoke volumes as to the level of worry he was harbouring, and I wondered how exhausted they all must feel by now, too.

'What did we miss?' Thompson asked as he threw his car keys onto the table.

Newell folded his arms and looked in on Edward, who was looking around his room with a decidedly bored expression fixed in place. 'Rule is talking to his doctor. She's had enough,' he ran a hand through his hair then, 'said she feels like he's taking the piss, holding us to a timeline. She wants to know what the state of play with his health actually–'

The door to our room banged open and Rule walked in in a fury.

'Good news then?' Kitsell asked.

'Everything he's said is true. Six months, more likely less.' Rule turned to fix me with a hard stare. 'Ask whatever you want, Maggie. Go off-script, get whatever you can...'

Having been given that new sense of freedom, I found there was nothing at all that I truly wanted to know. Edward had smeared and stained my life already. *Can I handle any more?* I thought as

I looked across to him, with his clasped hands and his set expression, the picture of neutrality while he explained to me that no, he didn't know what was wrong with him exactly, only that it had always been there.

'It was there in the playground, when we were kids?' I snapped back.

He smiled. 'Something was there.'

'But you hadn't done anything by then?'

Edward shook his head. 'I didn't do anything until years later.'

'Why?'

The question seemed to confuse him. 'I was a kid,' he made the answer sound obvious, 'I was hardly likely to leave school one day, murder a girl and then carry on with my O-levels, was I?'

'So when did you– I mean–' The sentences collapsed into ash in my mouth and I was desperate for tea, water, anything. 'Do you even remember when this started, really?' I managed to ask and he looked pleased with the question. I wondered whether he'd been waiting for this one.

'You never forget your first, Maggie.' He winked at me then. My dry mouth became drier still and, though I wouldn't give into the feeling, I was overcome with a desire to cry; a deep shoulder-shuddering outpouring that I felt the tug of already in my muscles. I opened my mouth to try to form an answer but Edward held up a finger to pause me. 'I'm not going to tell you about the first though. It was terrible, and I know everyone's is but truly, it was *terrible*, and I've tried to forget about it since.'

I couldn't marry what he was saying with how he was saying it, and I felt the weight of his remark settle heavy like a brace that enveloped my upper body. There was a great compression around my chest as my thoughts slipped into automatic and catapulted me back to the only first I had a frame of reference for: a cheap hotel room; the last day of school; the quiet agreement that we would love each other through the distance of our university years. It hadn't been terrible at all; it had been painful and laboured and awkward, but not terrible. And that same tsunami of tears rippled through me then, only this time I couldn't halt a few stray beads of feeling from escaping and landing hard on the table. In a tin room with no other sounds, the force of them against the cold metal caused an echo.

'I didn't mean our first time,' he said then, sullen in his speech.

'It doesn't matter, Edward.'

'Maggie, listen–'

'I said it doesn't matter,' I snapped, and the cut of my teeth was enough to quieten him. 'How close are we to the end?'

Edward was quiet for what felt like a prolonged period of time then. He turned around to check the clock, and I began to wonder whether he'd made a quiet deal with himself that he wouldn't speak again until the hour was over – or perhaps, wouldn't speak again until it was nearly over, giving him time enough to say what he pleased but not giving me time enough to question him about it. As though debunking those theories for me though, he spoke again when there were still fifteen minutes for me to question him in.

'Glasgow.'

I narrowed my eyes. 'That's the last place?'

'That's the last place you need for where I... Well, you know,' he said, suddenly bashful, modest. I could have slapped him for feigning such a set of feelings when everything up until now had been a vicious brag. 'Not the last place, really, but the first place–'

'I gathered,' I interrupted him. Edward had gone to university in Glasgow – which could only mean one thing, of course, which was that Edward had just told me where it began.

'But you're not going to tell me, tell them.' I nudged my head towards the mirror-window between us and the detectives. 'You're not going to tell any of us about your first?'

'I'm allowed to take *some* secrets to my grave.' He was no longer sullen, but had returned instead to his usual bite and sting. 'Besides, Glasgow might be where it happened, but that doesn't mean they'll find the girl.'

'Girl, or woman?'

He smirked. 'Haven't I given you enough?'

'You still haven't given me Lucy.'

Edward turned and caught sight of the clock again. There was hardly any time left for us. Five minutes at most, if the guard was late. I wanted to nudge him – right off the face of a cliff and into giving me an answer – but I knew that in this power-play dynamic Edward thought there was something valuable about his silence still; a shoestring it inevitably tied us all to. His demeanour made me desperate to seem unfazed by his quiet, but I'm sure we both knew better.

As though sensing the arrival of his escort, he smiled at me then, in the same instant that the door opened. The expression reached up to his eyes and I noticed for the first time – or perhaps, appreciated for the first time – the crow's feet denoting laughter and ageing and many other things we should have shared together, in place of him sharing them with fellow villains and inmates. Unable to resist, I found that my hand shot up to feel at the corner of my own eye. I was looking for braille markings that might show my own years of enjoyment. I perhaps shouldn't have been surprised when I didn't find any indentations there.

'Come on, Eddy, up you get,' the guard encouraged him.

'One second?' Edward gestured with a raised finger and though the other man rolled his eyes, he allowed it. Edward leaned across the table and spoke in a lowered voice. I thought it was for my benefit, a shared whisper from spouse to spouse as though there were a privilege in knowing this fresh and shiny detail, but I soon realised he wasn't only speaking to me; he was speaking *into* the recording device that lay between us. Head bowed, he looked up and made eye contact with me as he revealed the confession that had been the catalyst for so many others. 'Detective Rule, did it ever occur to you,' he paused and dampened his lips with the edge of his tongue, and it made him that bit more of a villain, 'did it ever occur to you that the reason I haven't told you about Lucy is because she isn't my secret to tell...'

TWENTY-FIVE

I told Kitsell that if I was going to be unwell then I was at least going to be unwell in my own bed, in my own home. He helped me to pack the mess of belongings that had migrated to the hotel with me, and then carted me back to my house, standing behind me with arms already outstretched, as though waiting for me to keel over on the path to the door. It was only a cold, the flu at most, but Kitsell had shifted into an overprotective gear, as though he'd been charged with guarding the case's most valuable asset, and I begrudged being tended to like I was a sickly woman in need of a hand. Though when a giddy spell whirled around me and left me reaching for the doorframe of the front door to steady myself, I realised I may have undercut my arguments somewhat when it came to whether I needed someone to stay with me.

'Why don't I call Finn?' Kitsell asked when I was safely sat at the kitchen table.

'Because he has better things to do.'

'Than take care of his mother?'

'Yes.'

There was a stretch of quiet while Kitsell waited for the

kettle to boil. He dropped a teabag into a mug and then crossed to the fridge, before tutting and–

'You haven't been here for weeks, Maggie, there's not even milk. Let me do a...' His sentence trailed off when the front doorbell echoed in from the hallway. 'Are you expecting someone?'

'Asda.' I struggled up from my seat, using the kitchen table as a support. 'If you could try to unpack the milk first, that would be helpful. Will you stay for a drink?'

Kitsell didn't have time for a drink, of course.

I'd said that I didn't have energy enough to confront Edward, despite us having a meeting scheduled. It was a decision that I felt a fresh wave of remorse for, but every dizzy spell and every chesty cough and every spit into the bathroom sink validated the decision as a sensible one. In my absence, Kitsell and Thompson had requested they have a meeting with Edward instead. They were part of the original investigating team, and I knew they had spoken to Edward prior to my involvement in this second movement of investigations, too. I wondered whether their meetings with him felt to them like a reunion of sorts – in a similar, sickening way to how mine had to begin with – but I hadn't had time to ask Kitsell before he'd set a cup of tea in front of me and told me he needed to go. Though he'd be back later, and he'd be bringing Thompson with him.

Time had moved slowly since. I had sipped my tea until the cup ran dry and I had managed to move through the first of my to-do lists – newspapers and webzines – to search for the boys' names again, but even the relief of not finding them wasn't enough to lift my spirits or boost my failing energy levels. While I waited for the kettle to sing to a boil I stared into the garden, as I had done on so many other easy mornings while brewing tea and considering work that needed to be done, but the mess and overgrowth of it no longer bothered me. I didn't know whether that was indicative of how sick I felt from the bug moving through my system, or whether, instead, it was evidentiary of how much my care for life had crumpled since this process with Edward had begun. The garden no longer seemed important.

When the water had boiled I decided against tea and made Lemsip in its place, the lemon steam rising and clearing my nose bit by bit, breath by breath at a time. I looked around to the open expression of my laptop on the table and the handful of papers I had managed to unpack and with a deep and husky sigh I thought, *I'd love for someone to make me soup.*

Though my appetite escaped me still, I decided that cooking could be both a kind and necessary distraction from imagining what might have been happening inside the prison at that time. I pulled free carrots and green beans and red onions from the salad store in the fridge, and a shiver moved through me as I closed the door after them. I couldn't regulate my temperature, but I refused to let that slow me as I hunted through the cutlery drawer for a vegetable peeler, feeling my way around the landscape that had somehow become alien to me in these short weeks – short weeks where so much had happened though, I reminded myself, feeling a dull elation when I finally laid my hand on the implement I needed.

It was a perfect, mindless repetition to skin a vegetable and set it aside; skin and set aside. By the time I'd moved on to cutting the vegetables into neat and uniform chunks, I had lost sense of where we were in the morning. I deliberately avoided looking at the clock. My watch was lying lifeless on the kitchen window, and I had left the radio mute, too, in case the news reports or weather warnings between panel discussions gave away my sense of place in the landscape of the day. I threw the medley of ingredients into a large pot with water and vegetable stock and set a kitchen timer to keep track of its slow progress. There was too much there for just me, and I wondered whether

Kitsell and Thompson would object to portions of soup ladled by a sick woman. I ferreted out Tupperware containers all the same and laid three bowls along the kitchen worktop, in case they had time and stomach to eat; or at least, stomach to take to-go servings with them. It was the closest I had felt to normal in longer than I could remember, despite the narrowing of my nasal cavities and the distortion of tastes, both of which only occurred to me when I tried to smell and sample my way through the soup that was simmering to a boil.

I resolved to leave it another ten minutes before setting it aside to cool and then, and only then, did I chance a look at the clock. *They'll be here any minute*, I realised. So I sat at the kitchen table with clasped hands and I stared into the garden and I listened to the heartbeat from the wall clock; faint though it had been throughout my peeling and chunking and chopping, it was an unavoidable sound now, so clear that it may have been coming from inside my own body.

The front doorbell was such an intrusion to this that I actually flinched at the sound. There was an echo of the ring in my ears as I trod along the hallway and forced a smile. I touched my eyes then, to see whether there were crow's feet framing them, and I was disappointed to pull away with empty fingertips again. Kitsell and Thompson didn't have crow's feet either, I had noticed, but when I opened the door to greet them both neither of them were smiling. Instead, they looked exhausted and troubled and–

'Would you like soup?' I spat the question out like a nervous answer to something they hadn't asked. 'I wanted something to keep my hands busy,' I said, only then realising that I was wringing them around each other.

While I had expected kindness from Kitsell, it had actually been Thompson that extended his warmth first. 'Soup would be great, Maggie. We'll both take some.'

Kitsell only nodded in agreement, his mouth a thin line drawn through his face. I wondered how bad it must have been, while feeling too terrified, too weary even to ask. Instead, I led them back towards the kitchen and I portioned soup into the three bowls that I had left waiting, and I told them inane details about the contents of our lunch – 'I thought of adding parsnips but...' – while the two men swapped uncomfortable looks between themselves at my kitchen table.

When I was seated with my own bowl in front of me Kitsell pulled something from his pocket and set it dead centre between us all. It was the tape recorder; *my* tape recorder.

'We need you to hear some of what was said today.'

I blew on a spoonful of soup that I didn't have the stomach to swallow. 'Okay.'

Thompson was already eating. *How desperate is he to busy himself?* I wondered. Meanwhile, Kitsell skipped the recording ahead to its necessary point before returning it to the table, and then he forced his way through his lunch, too. They both ate with a gusto that I couldn't understand, and certainly couldn't match – though of course, they already knew what was coming. I could only sit and listen, and wait.

'Lucy was a really nice girl, absolutely.' Edward's voice filled the room. 'You chaps must think so, too. You've been chasing her tail for years.'

There was a harsh and distinct difference between the tongue he used to speak to me and how he spoke to the former detectives. Edward sounded like a man chewing fat with two friends, far from the reality of what he was to them.

'We don't like loose ends,' Thompson's voice followed.

'How much will it kill you if you never find her?'

'We'll find her,' Kitsell answered.

'You might not.'

'What makes you doubt that we will?'

There was a long pause before Edward answered Kitsell's question. 'You haven't so far. It's been what, twenty years? Nearly twenty-one? All those girls and never Lucy. Maybe you should just write her off as—'

'We're not writing anyone off,' Thompson interrupted.

'Honourable one, your partner, isn't he?'

'That and more, and he's right, too. We're not going to give up looking for that girl.'

'Suit yourselves. You've done such a bang-up job finding these new ones, though, what are we up to now...'

I tuned out the number as he said it. His voice was a high screech, a chalkboard scratch, and I felt my shoulders tensed more the more I listened – the more callous he became with every comment.

Thompson set his spoon down in his bowl and dragged his lips across the sleeve of his jumper. He shouldn't have done, really; something so rich in colour was likely to stain. I opened my mouth to query the tape – *How much longer? What am I listening for?* – but he only held up a finger and jabbed in the direction of the recorder twice. I nodded my understanding and sank back against my chair. I tried to force a breath through my nose then but I couldn't expel anything, so instead I parted my lips and began pulling in air in hungry mouthfuls. I pushed my bowl away, too, sickened by the bulge and bob of vegetable chunks.

'Ed, this has been going on for so fucking long now.' Thompson in real-time winced at the curse word of Thompson on tape. 'Why don't you just cut the crap and tell us what the hell happened to Lucy?'

There was another long pause, disturbed by the sound of Kitsell's spoon knocking against the porcelain of the bowl as he dropped it to rest there. Edward made one, two noises of hesitation before he finally answered. 'Ask Maggie.' I heard a tapping sound in the background of his speech and I imagined his fingertips knocking the table as he said, 'I'll bet you if she thinks about it hard enough, she'll know.'

Kitsell leaned forward and clicked the pause button. 'So here we are, asking.'

I looked between the detectives once, twice and soon felt my stare turn into a sharp shake of my head because– *No,* I thought at a scream even though my voice proper felt as though it had been stripped clean out of me, *no, I don't know, I didn't, don't, haven't. I couldn't have known!* But from their expressions, I wasn't sure they were convinced anymore.

TWENTY-SIX

Lucy Scraggs was a twenty-one-year-old woman who was saving money to pay her way through university. She wanted enough money behind her to give herself a strong and fresh start in a new city, and she'd told her parents she thought it would take another year – but no longer – in order to set herself right in that position. Her parents didn't mind her still being at home though. Lucy was the Scraggs's only daughter and both mother and father were reportedly happy to have her there for a while longer, especially for such a good and adult reason, too. To raise this money, Lucy moved between childminding and tending the bar at a local public house. The childminding typically saw her work with two families on a regular basis throughout the average week, though there were occasional jobs she would take on, too, if her existing employers recommended her to someone. The bar work Lucy apparently enjoyed less, because while many men were respectful there were always some who weren't, and she found that she had to mention her father's name all too often to secure a safe distance between her and the drinkers; her father was known as someone with a fiery temper, though, so it paid to use his name occasionally.

Although Lucy was saving money, there were times when she chose to treat herself somehow, too, especially after a long stint at work. Nine days working without a day off wasn't uncommon for her. So spending the tenth day having afternoon drinks with friends, or treating herself to a manicure in the city never felt like excessive expenditure, and her parents encouraged that. Her friends would later comment how generous Lucy was with both her time and her money, and if a friend ever needed an ear or a pint, Lucy was purportedly the most reliable person to call. It was a reputation she never minded having.

Lucy went missing on a Saturday night in November. She had only told her parents that she was going out for a while – she was a young woman and they didn't question her – while she told her friends she was having a night at home. It was the first and only time, as far as evidence and testimony can tell, that Lucy had ever told such a lie. One friend said she had suspicions that Lucy had recently started to see someone, romantically, but there was nothing to substantiate this. Whether she was romantically involved with someone or not, Lucy left the house that evening having promised her parents she would be 'home at around the normal time'. There had already been whispers of missing girls but Lucy had promised her mother, during a private conversation before she left the house that night, that she would be careful and safe, and that nothing would happen to her.

But Lucy stepped free of her family home that night, and never came back.

Rule had called in advance to say they would be delivering some materials that might help the case to progress. After I had cried and wailed and convinced them that I truly didn't know anything – or if I did, then I didn't *know* that I knew – Rule decided the only way to discern whether Edward was right about my knowing was to place me in a situation that might tease something out. I hadn't known then that what she had really been orchestrating was two large box folders' worth of photographs, newspaper articles, clippings, statements–

'There's a lot of information here,' I narrated as I pulled apart the first box. I knew about Lucy – the dead woman who wasn't, owing to the missing body, the lack of closure, the lingering questions – but I wasn't sure I was ready to know *everything* of her, which looked to be what Rule (with the help of Newell and Kitsell) was encouraging me towards. 'What do I–' I shook the false start away. 'What is it you need me to do?'

Rule pinched her trousers at the knees and crouched. I was sitting on my living-room floor by then, one box having already spilled its innards over my dull cream carpet.

'I only need you to do what you've been doing throughout this *whole* thing,' she said in such a gentle voice that I wouldn't have been surprised if she'd reached up to push my greased hair back behind my ears, 'and that's to work out what we know, and what we might be able to use, to tie this case together. That's all we can keep on doing.'

I smiled and nodded and wondered for a second then whether she spoke to her children like this. They were probably too old now for her to be condescending to them *all* of the time, but Rule struck me as the sort of person who simply wouldn't be able to help herself, if only occasionally. I noticed, too, that she had resorted to using the old 'we' tactic, as though *we* were in this together, as though *we* were all going to see a room of our homes given over to documents and details relating to the woman a spouse had murdered. *Yes, detective, this is all* we *can keep doing,* I thought as I carried on pulling materials out of box one, only coming to an abrupt stop when my hand hit up against a collection of photographs, held together by a brown elastic band and wedged at the bottom of the container.

I wasn't ready to look Lucy in the eye; I wasn't sure I ever would be.

They swapped further pleasantries – what I needed to do, what they expected or hoped for – and then they left, leaving me alone with evidence of my husband's final betrayal. Though that wasn't altogether true, if Edward were to be believed; if Edward were to be believed, Lucy's disappearance – *not death*, I reminded myself, owing to this forever search – was someone else's. After hollow spaces and loud sighs, the rest of Edward's interview tape that Kitsell and Thompson had shared with me involved a steady stream of information from Edward, as though having so recently unearthed the shallow roots of a truth, he was determined to drag the full length of it out slowly. I grabbed a blank sheet of paper and a pen and, in place of my usual to-do list, I wrote out a list of everything I thought I knew insofar as Lucy and Edward, and the invisible creature that Edward now seemed determined to pin Lucy's demise to.

1. Edward knew Lucy, in passing, allegedly, owing to occasionally attending the same watering hole where she worked.
2. Edward had spoken to Lucy, in passing, to begin with.
3. Edward had established a friendship with Lucy.

'I *thought* about killing her, make no mistake in that...'

A strangled sound fell out of me as I remembered his admission on the tape. *My husband thought about killing the girl*, I thought to myself as though repetition would help me to acclimatise to the idea. Why it was so much more of a challenge to accept this one woman over the many others was beyond me. Perhaps Lucy was a blow too far, after so many blows recently that had, like an axe in a fairy tale, obliterated the precious cottage of memories I had managed to hold onto for so long. There was no longer a time Before Edward Did What He Did; now, there was only a time before I knew.

I forced out a long and slow breath before braving a swallow. The sound of it landed somewhere in my gut, and I kept writing.

4. Edward had fantasised about kil–

The bullet-point entry snapped in half before I could write it out in full.

5. Edward had invited Lucy into our home.

There was more, I was sure of it, but those felt like the most important points to carry into a search. And frankly, having written down anything more would have rendered me useless for further attempts at finding a seedling of truth in among the documents anyway. Each entry on the list felt how I imagined an actual bullet might; a piercing that was simultaneously slow and speed of light fast, cutting through the rubber of muscle fibres and tissue, landing in a crevice somewhere, too dangerous to remove but likely fatal if it remained there. When I thought of each entry in the list in such lethal terms, I wondered whether I could go through with this final test at all. *Pray God, let this be the final test* I thought as I shifted around leaves of paper, moving one pile of evidence to sit atop another before moving it back again.

With a critical eye – or as close to one as I could possibly manage – I started to look over the papers with the intention of making a second list. Anything that rang a bell or prompted a question or caused a rise of bile, I noted down with a number beside it. The list was sparse to begin with, the early paper shifts only revealing more information about Lucy and what a travesty it was for her to have been taken so soon, so much before her time. There were statements from friends, family, people who thought they saw her shortly before the disappearance and those who were convinced, and convincing, that they had seen her after, even though Edward had confessed to her murder by then.

Why though? I thought as I scanned his statement without reading it. I had heard enough of Edward's confessions first-hand by now; the prospect of reading another confession was too wearing, particularly if it had been made in vain. *Why confess to something you haven't done, Edward?* I wondered over and again as I started adding things to a Read pile, which did nothing to ease the overwhelming dread caused by looking at the To Read pile – which was still a box and a half big, hours into sitting on my living-room floor.

There was a forensics report that had explained Lucy's hair was found in the house. Two strands on the guest sofa in the living room, as it was then. It was a chance find, the police admitted, but a damning piece of evidence, too. Though given that Edward had easily admitted that Lucy had been in our home, all it really proved in my mind was that my husband had once been capable of telling the truth – when it suited him. Lies were more often his expertise, though, which of course, had rendered me here, I thought as I cradled my head in my hands and tried to force out a breath that didn't feel smashed-glass jagged.

That breath was a hard ask of my body, it seemed, with every shallow intake and exhale feeling like the precursor to tears. In truth, I was amazed I had held those back for quite so long already. Still, while my breathing remained laboured something else altogether began clicking into place, a mechanical whir and hum in the back end of my brain as though something had been replaced with a steam-punk fitment, strong enough to drag up memories that I thought had been buried in six foot of earth and then some. But one of the recollections reached out, stretched a proverbial hand beyond the grave and–

'I wasn't here the weekend that Lucy went missing,' I said aloud with actual surprise in my voice as though this were my first time realising it, rather than only my first time remembering...

***

It took two full days of searching. I ignored phone calls from Kitsell, Thompson and Rule. I even ignored a text message from Finn – *Just wanted to check in with you Mum xo* – and I trawled through time capsule after time capsule, one stacked atop another in boxes that had been moved from one attic or loft space to the next over the years. It was a curse of hoarding that I had inherited from my own mother – *So there were some things about her that were passed down to me...* – that had rendered me incapable of throwing away anything with a modicum of sentiment attached to it.

Twenty-two years ago, a friend who had slipped from my life – Barry Campbell – was diagnosed with cancer. He was young and his chances of survival were strong, but it was going to take a vicious amount of treatment to get him there. His wife, Dorothy, had barened a kind woman who would have helped anyone and they, like us, had two young boys running around their home. They were more my friends than they were Edward's, though that could have been said of most people we knew. Unless they were drinking companions or work colleagues, they were always more my friends. That's why, I supposed, when it came to helping out the Campbell clan it had been more a task that fell to me singularly than it did fall to us as a family, or Edward and I as a unit. There were some weeks where it felt as though I saw more of Barry and Dorothy's boys than I did my own. I often offered to host sleepovers, or attend sleepovers sometimes, reading the boys to sleep while Barry battled another unexpected overnight visit to a hospital ward. Dorothy hated to leave his side and I always understood that; I would have been the same with my own husband. Though of course, that stab of feeling only made me think of my husband now, lying in his prison cell, calling out for more painkillers, more of this, more of that. Edward had accepted his death sentence readily, I'd come to realise; Barry never accepted his.

I licked a fingertip and turned the leaf of another diary page. It had been Duncan's birthday, the youngest of their boys, and they were attempting to hold a birthday party for him at the house; despite the fact that it coincided with a treatment day for Barry. He'd been desperate to give his son an evening of normal life though, so I had again too keenly offered to help however I could. I'd asked Edward if he wanted to come – 'A kid's birthday party? No thanks,' he'd scoffed, and I could remember his reaction all too well, remember it stinging me to see that selfish streak so pronounced in him. Dorothy had told me to bring my boys along with me all the same, though, and we could make a proper boys' night of it all, once the rest of the rabble had gone. I lifted over another page in the diary, read and remembered how I'd check the boys' diaries – no sleepovers, no football matches or other sports events that had them fixed to the house for the weekend – but still, neither of them had wanted to come. It had been Otis who decided first and small Finn who had followed suit with his older brother, as he would have done for most things during that time.

I closed the diary and remembered with a start of realisation, as though again this were the first time I had realised something pertaining to the case. 'The boys had been at home the weekend that Lucy went away...'

Did other people know?

TWENTY-SEVEN

Sarah had redecorated her meeting room. The outside of the building went unchanged, but the innards of her space were now sleek and cold, neat. Walls that were previously soft and warm were white and bare, with black and charcoal-grey wall-hangings. The large picture frames were empty still, and the flowerpots hollowed. I wondered what she could possibly be planning to grow there that might complement the new feel. I imagined hard-edged succulents. If I'd known she was planning a change then I would have brought her one, not quite as a new home gift but certainly a new space one, given that the changes felt so drastic I initially felt like I'd stepped into an entirely different room to usual. Somehow, the area no longer felt fit for purpose, particularly given that she was making soft noises and cooing me into explaining why I was there.

Sarah had had to answer a panicked request from me again, though this time it had been a phone call rather than an email. That choice of contact had, I thought, likely given her an additional tip regarding the exact level of distress I was battling against. Faced off with the prospect of sharing it, though, I found that all I could now do was look around her new-old room and list the differences I saw, even though I didn't have a piece of paper to write anything down on. I'd have to try hard to remember them and note them down when I was home, then they could be added to the lists of other inane details that had occupied my days since– *Well, since,* I thought with a hard swallow. My to-do lists had been replaced with anything, everything that served as a distractor task until eventually I had simply run out of *things,* which left me with no other option, it felt at the time, than turning to the list of people who I could call. Kitsell and Thompson had been there, but Sarah, Otis, Finn, even Edward had been above them, which I thought spoke volumes to the distress, too. Out of my top five, Sarah had been the safest – but now I was here, all I could do was use her as another distraction, one that I was paying for the privilege of. Though the eight-five pounds I had transferred her already for this appointment helped to assuage my guilt at not saying anything; at least she was making something from this encounter, whether I found courage enough to use my voice or not.

Sarah parted her lips and pulled in a mouthful of air as though readying to speak, but when I waited her out, stared at her for a moment, she only smiled. It was that same thin-lipped and awkward expression that so many people seemed to wear now – or at least, so many people seemed to wear it around me. If I concentrated, I could superimpose Rule's face onto the woman in front of me and there would have been no difference between their sympathetic glances.

'I'm sorry,' I said eventually, 'this is a waste of your time.'

That, at least, gave her something to latch onto.

'It isn't a waste of my time to help someone, Maggie.'

'But I'm not telling you what's wrong,' I answered, 'I'm only sitting here and looking at your redecorated room.'

She laughed then, a soft and gentle crack appearing in our tension. 'It's not finished.'

Thank God, I thought but of course, didn't say. 'No?'

'These white walls are hideous, aren't they?' she said and I forced myself not to answer; it would have been rude to agree. It may have been a trap. 'I thought they'd be clean, or fresh, or... something other than the garish shade it actually seems to be. Off-white would have been better, but that always sounds dirty, doesn't it?' She laughed again and I managed to match the gesture that time, because of course, she was right. Off-white was the collar colour that our mothers had taught us to avoid. 'I'm going paint shopping this weekend.'

'I'm sure you'll choose something...' I pierced my lips together and searched for the right word. 'Softer?'

'Yes, softer,' she agreed, 'that's the colour I'll be aiming for.'

A long ten seconds passed then where it became clear that we had exhausted our well of small talk. Not quite a well, though, but more a puddle; something we anticipated being deeper that turned out to be only a small dip in the pavement.

'I think I'm a bad person,' I finally said, with such an abruptness that the words knocked together on their way out of my mouth. I actually reached a hand up to check my teeth were intact following the admission. 'I think no matter how much good I do, I'll never be a good person.'

Sarah's expression loosened into a lazy frown; her forehead was wrinkled, but there was a smile still fixed, too. 'Maggie, we've talked about this before.'

'Could we talk about it again, please?' My tone was pleading, and something about that encouraged a turn in her mood. She nodded and flashed a wide-handed gesture, as though physically welcoming whatever contribution I had to offer into the room with us. 'If someone is a bad person, can they ever be good?'

Sarah narrowed her eyes at the grey area. 'I think the real question is, is anyone ever *just* a bad person? Now I realise,' she shifted in her seat, made herself comfortable, and she seemed to concentrate hard on whatever was coming next, 'I realise there are extreme examples of badness in the world, and there are people that largely seem... I don't know, largely seem like they can't be redeemed, let's say. But if we ignore those extreme examples for a moment, is anyone ever *just* good or bad?'

I shook my head and repeated her question, but something caught in my tooth. 'Extreme examples of badness?'

'Maggie, are you about to tell me that you've murdered someone?'

A red heat crept up my neck. I wondered whether it was visible, whether the burn of it would soon appear over the top of my jumper as it became more widespread, taking over my face, my hands even. But when I looked down at my skin if anything my hands were paled, the only pinkish tinge something that could be explained away by this new tic of wringing my hands that I had acquired in the past few days, my fingers constantly twitching with an 'Out damned spot' demeanour as though it were impossible for them to be still. *The Devil makes work for idle hands, remember*, I thought as I tried, tried to hold them steady in my lap. I managed to shake my head in answer to Sarah's question, but I couldn't bring myself to force a verbal answer for fear of what else might come tumbling free of my open mouth.

'Murdering someone would be an extreme example of badness.'

I swallowed the beginnings of an animal sound that I felt rising in my throat.

'And even then, there are probably circumstances that would allow for it.' She made an awkward noise. When I looked up at her, I realised it was a laugh. 'Allow for is probably the wrong expression to have used there, but you take my meaning.'

I nodded. 'I understand.'

'You aren't a bad person, Maggie.'

The noise came out like a hiccup; louder than a hiccup, though, closer to a belch, and as though the sound had been acting as a cork for something, all of the feeling poured out of me after that. My eyes began to sting and stream, and my shoulders rolled and shuddered with the seeds of tears that slowly crept out of me, before flooding all at once as though a further cork had been removed. It was the first time I'd cried in days, although there had been many times when I'd thought I might. I couldn't remember the last time when I'd *felt* like a good person, though, in the core of myself, in the heart of me. To hear someone say that I was almost felt unbearable; it almost felt like pain.

Sarah reached beneath the table and pulled out a box of tissues that she then handed to me. She gave me a second or two of quiet while I dabbed at my eyes. It was times like these when I felt especially grateful for my blank slate of a face. There were no tracks of mascara, no lipstick to neaten. But there were feelings for me to dab at all the same; small overspills of emotion that snuck out from the corner of each eye.

'People don't normally react like that when they're given that reassurance,' she observed with a sad but sympathetic smile. 'Is there anything that's prompted this string of worries, do you know, anything we might be able to talk about in more detail?'

I kicked my toes at the fringes of the truth. I was desperate to talk to someone who wasn't part of an official policing body – or hadn't been, at some time in their lives. But policing bodies, parole boards, they were the only people that knew the truth of it all. Short of knowing that I had had a marriage that ended under terrible and painful circumstances, that led to name changes and relocations galore, Sarah knew nothing of my past life. That's how it felt, too, like a past life; something I had lived before living again, but I couldn't shake the residual energy of it all. Though Edward had made it non-residual, I supposed; he'd made it corporeal a second time over.

I shook my head. 'I've been going through a lot of old memories, sorting through boxes that have been stashed in the loft for years, those sorts of things.' I shrugged and dabbed at my eyes again. I wasn't even sure whether I was crying anymore. 'It brings up good things, of course, but...'

'It can bring up a lot of bad, too,' Sarah finished and I mumbled in agreement. 'I think, when we're looking back at memories like that, from a very distant part of our lives, it can be worth remembering that we're effectively looking at a different person, or a different version of ourselves at least. Which I know is very easy for me to say,' she said with a huff of a laugh, 'but who we are now is not who we might have been when we were in school, for instance, or we might have been when we were married.'

My head snapped up at the mention.

'These bad feelings,' Sarah pushed, 'might they have anything to do with your ex-husband?'

'I think they have *everything* to do with him,' I admitted. I tore small chunks free from the dampened tissue and let them collect in my lap. 'It's made me think a lot about our sons, too, I suppose. Looking back through family holidays, pictures from when the boys were younger. I've been thinking...' I forced out a long and slow breath that stuttered with feeling. 'I've been thinking a lot about the things I've got wrong, in my time, as a mother.'

Sarah frowned. 'Is there something specific you're referring to here?'

I pressed my lips together hard to seal in a confession and shook my head instead.

'In which case, if there's nothing we can attribute these bad feelings to, necessarily, perhaps we can put them in our feelings box for now, and this is something we can think about considering in more detail when we next see each other?' Sarah leaned forward to collect her diary from the table. 'If you'd like to schedule in another session?'

Over my years with Sarah, I had realised the so-called feelings box served two main functions. The first was that it provided me with a space – a space that felt physical and therefore more secure – to trap stray feelings in, until such a time that I felt better equipped to deal with them. Its second function, which had taken me longer to determine, was that it allowed Sarah to gently signal the end of a session without her overtly stating that my allotted time was up. It was a kinder method than simply checking her watch and telling me it was time to leave – but their eventual effects were the same.

'Could I see you next week?'

'Of course, Maggie. Same day, same time?'

I nodded and concentrated on collecting the tissue flecks that were scattered along my jeans. 'Thank you.'

Sarah scribbled something into next week's diary space, closed the book and then smiled across at me. 'Between now and next week, I'd like you to spend some time thinking about why you're a *good* person, Maggie.' She held up her hand to pause me; I hadn't even started to make a rebuttal, but she must have sensed one was likely. 'I don't need an extensive list. One or two things, starting with, I've been a good mother. Treat it like an affirmation, at least one a day.'

'I've been a good mother,' I repeated with a forced smile, and Sarah seemed pleased by that. On my way out of the room I tipped a palmful of tissue scraps into the bin and repeated quietly, inwardly, *I've been a good mother.* I took the stairs back to the ground level and pushed my way out onto a busy street. *I've been a good mother.* There was a shopping list burning a hole in my pocket that I decided to tackle on the way home, too. *I've been a good mother.* But somewhere between Sarah's office and the supermarket entrance, I saw three newsstands with their sandwich boards boasting headlines that could only possibly be about Edward and just like that – *I've been a bad mother.* – the ugly truth of it all came flooding back.

TWENTY-EIGHT

I wrote the text with a tone of confidence that was not only uncharacteristic but entirely feigned – *I'm coming over this afternoon. 5.30. It's best if we're left alone.* – and then I hit send before I had flailing doubt enough to second-guess my decision. I had tried calling in the days since I had seen Sarah; I had left messages both stern and pleading. But all of the calls had gone unanswered and all of the messages were unreturned. I wasn't sure how anyone could, in good conscience, ignore quite so many calls from one single person who was very clearly going to *some* effort to get in touch – until I started to treat Kitsell with the same unwise courtesy. He had been phoning me, on behalf of Rule, Newell, and their wider team I guessed, and he had left voicemails, too, that I had not only not responded to, I'd not even listened to them, knowing that it would crack my resolve.

Unfortunately, Kitsell was not only being gifted with the same treatment I was – the ghost-like non-answers in the face of someone you're trying to contact – but he was treating me with the same treatment, too, and a smarter woman may have anticipated that coming. Regrettably, though, I was not a smarter woman. So when the doorbell chirped midway through my morning writing, I thought nothing of rushing to the other side of the house to greet what I assumed would be the postman, with a bundle of research books. Far from a bold red uniform and wide smile, though, Kitsell was there in a brown and beige ensemble, just about visible from underneath a coat that looked large enough for a family of three to camp in. He didn't smile, only nodded, and I knew then that I was in more trouble than I'd expected to be.

'You'd better come in.' I stepped aside and he wordlessly entered the hallway, wiping his feet with purpose on the mat before treading the length of the hall. There were still clumps of mud that shed from the tread of his shoes as he walked, but I tried very hard not to let the smear of it bother me – at least until he was gone.

'You're cooking,' he commented when I joined him in the kitchen.

'I'm making batches of soup for the food bank, among other things,' a nervous laugh escaped me, 'you're welcome to a Tupperware container, if you want to take something for your...' I petered out when Kitsell held up a hand and shook his head lightly. His expression wasn't unfriendly, but it lacked the warmth that it might once have had, too. *I deserve that, I suppose*, I thought, given the tally of attempts to contact me. 'Can I get you a drink?'

'Do you have herbal tea?'

'Of course,' I rushed to the cupboard, 'peppermint, fruit, I have this orange and–'

'Peppermint is great, thank you.'

I heard the squeal of a seat being pulled back from the table. But I concentrated only on filling the kettle, sourcing cups, and making a mammoth task of deciding whether I wanted tea or coffee for myself. I held the caddy for each of them, one in each hand, as though I were literally weighing up their contents.

'Rule thinks you've remembered something.'

The coffee caddy slipped from my hand and clanged against the work surface. I took that to be a decision, and I stashed it back inside the cupboard before dropping a breakfast teabag into my mug. I put a peppermint bag into Kitsell's guest mug and turned to face him while the kettle boiled. It was hard to look at him, but I was sure that avoiding his glance would only make me seem that bit more– *guilty?*

'Thompson and I have fought your corner.' He wasn't looking at me as he spoke. Instead, he was appraising the work materials that I'd left strewn across the table. 'We've both said, Maggie isn't the sort to hide things from us. She didn't before and she wouldn't do now.' He moved a sheet of paper, stared at the one beneath it and then moved it back. I wondered whether he was expecting to find notes relating to the case, or to Lucy – or at the very least, relating to something more interesting than Level 2 Plumbing, which was the course I'd been contracted to write for a local college. 'And you wouldn't, would you?' The kettle clicked and his head shot up; he stared at me with a narrowed view, and I felt my skin prickle all over.

I shook my head. 'I haven't remembered anything.' I told myself it wasn't a lie. 'I haven't been well, I– Well, it's not that I haven't been well, physically, exactly, physically I'm fine but I– Things have been hard, *it* has been hard to– Going back over it all and reading– Lucy's file, it's not easy reading and I–'

It was easy for me to sound fractured, troubled. That's how I'd felt for days and, truthfully, it was at the very least a contributing factor to why I'd ignored Kitsell's calls. He bought it, too, I thought, given that he was up and out of his seat before I could finish my strangled explanation of things. Kitsell set a hand on the ball of my shoulder and ducked his head into my line of vision. I'm not sure I even realised he was out of his seat until then.

'I'm going to tell Rule you're still working through things, trying to piece things together. Does that seem fair?' I managed a nod. 'I'll give you a call in a couple of days.' Kitsell gestured to the boiled kettle behind me. 'I'll give that tea a miss, I think. But I'll be in touch soon.'

'I'll answer,' I promised.

'It would be helpful for me if you did,' he said in a tone that nearly sounded light-hearted, though from his expression it was clear that wasn't how he felt. 'I'll see myself out then, and I'll call in a few days,' he reiterated. Kitsell was nearly out of the room when he turned back in to face me. Whatever was coming, he looked to measure the words carefully before saying them aloud. 'You owe that man *nothing*, Maggie, I'd like you to remember that.'

I forced a smile. 'I can assure you, I'm unlikely to forget it.'

But there are other men in my life to whom I owe a great deal...

***

The house was a wasteland. The car that should have been on the drive wasn't. There were no lights on either, no warmth to the building. It didn't matter how many times I rang the doorbell. It was all too apparent that no one was home, despite my forewarning – or maybe because of it. I trod back to the car and climbed into the driver's seat. The small vehicle was a capsule of smells, with containers of soup, lasagne, and home-made cookies resting in rows along my back seat. I had planned this visit in line with my food bank delivery, hoping that the pressure of a time limit – I had imagined being able to say, 'I can't stay long.' – would have made us both more likely to talk, more likely to rush the information out in a string of reveals rather than a slow-burn of them. I had had too much time to sit with the realities of the Lucy paperwork already, and I hadn't been especially keen to give myself too long in lingering over its inevitable climax. But the idea had fallen flat, it seemed. There were no missed calls, no text messages. I hit the dial button and pressed the phone to my ear but, rather than it ringing through to a voicemail service again, it cut directly to a message informing me that my call couldn't be connected at all. I wondered whether the handset had been turned off – or whether he would have gone to the extreme of blocking me altogether, which wouldn't necessarily have been a surprise by then.

I typed another message – *Please call me.* – and hit send. I had no need or desire for confidence by then. I only wanted this over with.

I waited a minute, two minutes, in case a reply rushed in; in case he mightn't have just not had signal enough for a phone call. But nothing came, and I soon gave up hope. I started the car, shifted it into gear and pulled away. It was only a ten-minute drive to the food bank from there, but it felt as though the journey ran on automatic. I pulled into a space not knowing whether I had stopped at red lights or adhered to speed limits; I could only hope I had managed both.

There were three large bags to unload from my back seat and such is the British way, I was determined to carry them all in a single and swift journey. I was struggling to balance the final of the bags, though, and there was an influx of relief when a hovering voice – 'Let me help you with those.' – came to the rescue from somewhere behind me. It was a young man, no older than a teenager, at a push, though I thought he may have been younger. It wasn't until I looked up and saw his mother, waiting just a few steps away, that I realised who he was. The eldest son from the family of three that I'd smuggled grocery monies to. Only now, it was a family of two.

The mother smiled. 'Nice to find a gentleman in the world, isn't it?'

'Mum...' he groaned with some embarrassment. But still, he eased another one of the three bags away from my grasp, leaving me with only the soup containers to carry. 'Honestly, I can manage the second one,' he said to me with a tired smile.

'One of those bags has got cookies in,' I answered, 'I dare say that Claire will let a helper have first pick, if you carry them into the centre for her.'

His smile widened. 'In which case, I can definitely manage the two.'

The mother fell into line to walk with me, while I held the final bag between two hands, my torso hidden behind the hemp of it as though the delivery were a shield. I was desperate to ask where her youngest son was, but something in me was nervous of an answer.

'He's rushing now he knows there'll be a cookie in it for him,' she joked and nodded ahead to the boy who was nearing the doors of the food bank already. We were lingering behind, neither of us in a hurry. 'I'm glad to see you again,' she said quietly then, keeping the conversation between the two of us, 'I wanted to thank you, for what you did for us the other week, with the– Well, with the money.'

'You thanked me.' I smiled without looking at her. I was all too aware that a direct gaze might make her feel awkward, but I hoped she might see the expression from my profile. 'But you're welcome.'

'The boys, they were really grateful for it, too.'

I sucked in a hearty breath then, the precursor to my question. 'Your other son...'

'Isn't with us today.'

'No.'

A long silence stretched out between us as we closed the

distance to the doors. I wanted to ask more, wanted to probe under the cover of her silence. But I realised, too, the uncomfortable likelihood that I was making my situation into her situation – or perhaps, hers into mine. By the time we arrived at the doors proper I felt such a swell of sickness rise in me that I thought I wouldn't be able to go through with the evening's shift at all; not knowing that somewhere in the room there was a former family of three, not knowing either the circumstances under which the third wheel of the family had tumbled loose, even though I knew I had no business in knowing.

'I'm so sorry,' I lowered the bag to the ground, 'I've just remembered I left something in the car. Would you mind taking this in for me?'

'Oh, of course not, no.' She reached for the handles. 'I'll just leave it…'

'Just into the reception. Claire will take it from there.'

I waited until the doors opened and swallowed her whole before I rushed back to the car. The stench of food that was left over in the vehicle only worsened the sickness. I clicked for cold air to rush from the vents inside, but I lowered both the driver's and passenger side windows, too, and I gulped in air hungrily the whole way home. The driveway felt like a haven. I pulled the car in and killed the engine in such a hurry that it was more a stall than a smooth stop, and then I threw the door open with equal urgency, convinced that I couldn't keep the sickness at bay any longer. It would only be coffee, I reminded myself, as though that were some consolation. *It will only be coffee and then it will be over; it will only be—*

'Mum?'

I willed for my head to snap up but instead it was a slow rise. I was still half-hanging out of the door, staring up at my son now who looked as sick as I felt. His typically tanned complexion was paled and his eyes were darkened in a way that made him look like his father, and that thought sickened me all the more. *Like father, like son; like father, like–*

'Mum, are you okay?'

He cut the thought off and I was thankful for that at least. But I couldn't answer his question. Because of course, I wasn't okay. Because nothing about this was okay...

TWENTY-NINE

When Otis was thirteen years old, he went into my bedroom and searched through my chest of drawers until he found my emergency money. It had never been a secret. Both of the boys had known there was money there, though I'd never given them a specific drawer to search in exactly. I'd always told them, though, that if they ever needed money and I wasn't at home, they should go to the chest of drawers and take whatever they needed – providing they told me afterwards. I had always imagined it would be takeaway pizza when I'd been running late home from work; settling a bill with a plumber if I happened to be out of the house when he'd called for his fee; buying a magazine from a charity worker when they'd knocked on the front door. None of these situations had ever happened. Whenever there had been a takeaway night it was always the three of us; I never let a bill fester; charity workers were few and far between in every area we lived in. When Otis had taken the money, it had been for a different reason altogether.

His friends were going for food and then going to the cinema; or the cinema and then food. Regardless of the ordering, Otis's pocket money only extended to the one activity and he was pained deeply by the denial of one or the other. He asked for extra money one week and I remember asking whether he'd mow the garden for me. I didn't like the idea of handing money out for nothing – which was dangerously close to the arrangement of their weekly allowance anyway. I had always promised myself that if the boys needed extra, they would have to do extra to earn it. Otis had called it 'child labour' and said I was 'exploiting' his needs by even asking.

'Exploiting your need for money?'

'Well yeah, Mum, obviously.'

'Right.' I'd thought long and hard about how to answer that accusation. 'You're going to struggle a touch when it comes to a job, sweetheart.'

Nothing more was said on the matter. When Otis disappeared for a full day the weekend after, I'd assumed that a friend had kindly offered to buy his food, or his cinema ticket – or even that the plans had changed altogether, such was often the case with kids of that age. But the plans hadn't changed. Otis had gone to the cinema and to the restaurant afterwards, and he'd paid for himself at each. And he'd been off school with a vicious sickness for three days straight after that day.

It was on the fourth day that he came into the living room and asked me to sit down, so he could talk to me. I had been in the middle of ironing school uniforms, and I'd made him wait until I'd finished the collar of one of Finn's shirts before I sat opposite him on the sofa. My sickly son, with his paled skin and puffy cheeks, had stared hard at the carpet, an inch or two away from where my feet were, and confessed.

'I took thirty pounds from the emergency money upstairs.'

Now, two decades on, he wore the same sickly expression. Otis was sitting on the guest sofa and staring intently at the floor. After I'd let us both in I offered him tea, soup, a cookie, even, and he'd declined everything and said he had a nervous stomach, a problem that I recognised as being distinctly Otis. He may have been hard-edged the majority of the time, especially these days, owing to his work, but when something scored into my son it ran deep – and he could never hold himself steady for long.

I set a glass of water on the small table alongside his seat, and then I crossed to sit in my armchair. I'd brought a glass of water for me, too, though it was largely a prop; something to busy myself with, if such a time came that I needed a distraction from anything my son was about to say. But for a long time he didn't say anything. The only noise between us was the incessant tick-tick of the clock on the mantelpiece. After six minutes – *six!* – I wondered how much I would miss it if I were to grab the thing from its shelf and fling it into the garden, where my to-do list was becoming more unruly, thorn-pricked and sodden.

But on the seventh minute Otis cleared his throat. 'Did Dad tell you?'

My son couldn't look at me. But I couldn't look away from him.

Of course, in Edward's own perverse and manipulative way, he'd told me everything I needed to know – or at least, led me to everything I needed to find, in order that I might guess. Edward had spent our entire life together dancing around truths; a two-step of did-this-happen or was-it-really-this. Telling me about our son had been no different, now. The bastard had led me here; to this belly-aching moment of realising that even after I had left my husband – *even after my husband had left me*, I corrected – there had still been a killer living in my home.

I swallowed and the thud of it landed like a small stone against the back of my throat. *Do I answer as his mother, or do I answer as a woman sitting at the feet of a murderer?*

'I think you always knew that he would, sweetheart.'

Like a summertime flower caught in winter rain, my son folded in on himself then. Otis's shoulders bunched forwards, his head dipped, and he sobbed in a way that I have only ever seen him do once before: the day he found out about Edward. I understood, now, that Edward's confession had been a double-pronged jab at my son, that he had carried the wounds of for twenty years. Now, they were weeping over my living-room carpet; years of badness and untreated infection spilling out and he sobbed and sobbed with the pain of it until listening to his jagged breaths became too much to stand and I found I was kneeling in front of him then. I pulled his head towards my shoulder, and I shushed and cooed in a way that I can't have done for over twenty years. It would have been a knee graze or a broken toy or perhaps even the announcement that Otis would soon be getting a little brother, which was not news that he took particularly well. And with that stab of memory I found I was asking the one question that I was truly terrified to know the answer to.

'Does Finn know?'

Otis shook his head against me. He leaned back then and put a small distance between us; enough for us to see each other's faces. Mine, impassive and smooth and rehearsed; his, blotchy and tear-stained and wrinkled like a bulldog's. 'No one knows, Mum, you're the first– You and Dad, you're the only people who know.' He dropped back against me and continued to spill his heartache. Meanwhile, I rubbed at his back and kissed the crown of his head and I promised that things would be fine, whatever happened, knowing that that perhaps wasn't true, but not knowing what other parents' lie I might balm his wound with. Because of course, reacting like a parent – like a forgiving parent, who would always be on the side of their child no matter the crime – that reaction was the only choice I had. Surely. After everything that Edward had inflicted on his sons, how could I give Otis anything other than the confessional he needed to ease this old upset? That was what I told myself, then, that was what I *had* to tell myself, I realised. There was no other way; no other way around.

You and Dad, you're the only people... I thought over and again as I tried to soothe our son. It occurred to me in those troubled moments that Edward had perhaps been a better father than I had allowed him credit for; perhaps we had been a better team than I realised. I wondered whether Edward had known, or at the very least believed that all along; whether his firm faith in that belief, perhaps, was why he'd told me now, or at the very least structured a situation wherein I might find out for myself, what our son had done. Or perhaps Edward had only decided that was one too many secrets to take to his grave.

Like father, like son I thought then, a bee-sting nipped at the back of my head, and a strangled sound slipped out of me. Otis seemed not to have heard. *Like father, like–*

The thought chased its tail around my brain, a dog, caged for too long and now suddenly released, it was rowdy and loud and uncontrollable. And it made it near-impossible to focus, to think of anything to say, even. Because what was there to say? This wasn't petty cash from the bedroom drawers. This was a woman's life. I swallowed hard again and blinked back the harsh bite of tears forming. *This was my son.*

I had to wait a long time for the animal wail of Otis to ease. It rocked his whole body, each sob seeming to take more and more energy for him to move through, until eventually he slumped, as though relaxing into the relief of his confession. And I wondered whether that's what it was, a quiet relief; that someone else now knew, that someone else could now carry this with him. *But why did that someone have to be me?*

'I need to know what happened, Otis,' I eventually said. Though truly I didn't, and I would have guessed that he would rather not tell me. But if my husband had taught me anything, it was that to lie well you needed to know the absolute truth of a situation. So I sat back on my heels, and I cupped my son's knees with my sweating palms, and I begged for the absolute truth.

'I don't know how much I remember, Mum, honestly, I–'

'Well, then I need as much as you can remember. Can you give me that much?'

He nodded and wiped at the drip of his nose with the sleeve of his jumper, and just like that he was a boy again. 'I really didn't mean to do it, Mum, I really...' he petered out as the cries gathered in his throat again.

'What you meant doesn't matter,' I snapped, sounding sharper than I meant to. But didn't he deserve the scolding? Didn't he deserve a harsher punishment than being barked at by his mother? 'What you did is what mattered. Can you give me that?'

He nodded again and avoided my stare; his eyes settled on the carpet somewhere to the side of me. 'I found her in the living room and... things had been bad with you and Dad, like, you hadn't been talking as much and... I don't know, Finn and I, we both felt like we hadn't been together as much. Then you went away for the weekend and there was this woman, this young bloody woman just lolling about on our sofa.' In place of his tears, I saw anger clamber onto its haunches – and I saw his father in him then, too. But Otis's rage died quickly enough, the pilot light on a heater fading, as he remembered, or perhaps realised, what he'd seen hadn't been what he thought he saw. 'I thought he'd brought her there to cheat on you,' he admitted, his shoulders sagging as he made the admission aloud. 'I don't even know... I can't even remember *thinking*, never mind remember *what* I was thinking. I was just so angry at her and at him and– I thought he was going to hurt you!'

Otis looked at me then, truly looked at me, with wide pupils and tears in his eyes still, and I felt a fresh new fracture break down the centre of my heart.

'So you killed her?'

'So I killed her.'

The groan was guttural. I felt it as much as I heard it; the turn of my stomach, the grind of something misshapen against the walls of my belly. There was the bite of acidity in the back of my throat and I wondered whether vomiting was inevitable; whether it was natural, in a situation like this one. *Is anything about this situation even remotely natural?* But there was no stock response, I knew that, too. There was no easy way to contend with your child transforming before your very eyes, morphing into the monster beneath the bed that you had spent years warning him of, unaware, so comfortably unaware, that he, too, was a kind of monster. Though that was another uncomfortable thought; one that caused a strike of guilt to shoot through my spine and I felt myself stiffen. My stomach groaned again. My son was a monster. And I loved him so dearly, still.

'And then what happened?' I asked.

Otis looked as though I'd presented him with an unsolvable problem, a riddle with no tail. I recognised the expression from when he was stumped with his maths homework as a child, and I remained steadfast in my reply that he'd need to work the answer out for himself. It tortured me, that memory of him, infantilised. *He was already a killer by then,* I reminded myself, and that knowledge sat at an awkward angle, at odds with the fondness, with the warmth of Otis challenging himself to be better, learn more, work harder. Now, he shook his head, squinted, and tried to form a word but nothing came. I brushed stray flecks of hair back behind his ears; it really needed to be trimmed and I wondered whether he was too old for me to tell him so. I cupped his face in my hands to fix his stare to me and I spoke slowly then, as though I were speaking to the boy who committed the murder, not the man confessing to it.

'After you killed her, what happened?'

Otis only shook his head again. 'I don't know, Mum.'

'You mean you can't remember that part?'

'No, I mean I just don't know.'

I felt my forehead pull together in the confusion of it all. 'After–'

'I understand what you're asking me, Mum,' he snapped, sounding more like his own self. But there came a deep swallow and a shaky breath before he explained. 'But I'm telling you I don't know. Dad, I think he saw, he might have watched.' Otis pulled away from me and worried at his temples with his fingertips. 'I think he watched and then after, he told me to go back to bed. He said he'd fix it. He gave me milk.'

I swallowed back rising bile. 'He gave you milk?' The detail snagged in my teeth.

'I don't know what he did with her, Mum. I've never known, I...' Otis let his sentence die half-formed, but after another slow and shaky inhale, he managed to breathe enough life back into it. 'I don't know what he did with Lucy, Mum, I don't...'

After all this, I thought as I rubbed softly at the crown of my boy's hair, while he rested his forehead against me, *after all this, and I still can't tell that girl's parents where she is...*

THIRTY

My son regressed that evening. Like a teenager caught short, he asked me to call his girlfriend and lie for him – 'Can you just tell her I've fallen asleep? Please, Mum?' – and then shortly after that, he moved from teenager to boy. He fell asleep on the sofa with his head in my lap while I ran my fingers through his hair and retold him stories from mine and his father's youth. He asked to know about us when we were younger and after the hours of crying sandwiched around his confession, I didn't have it in me to deny him that comfort. So I told him how Edward and I met, even though he must have known the story already, and I told him how we parted ways for a short while, while we were both at university; I did not tell him that that is when his father killed for the first time, I did not tarnish the memories of family holidays that I revisited with him hours later. I was glad when I felt his breathing change, a sign that he'd slipped into sleep, so I could enjoy my own– *Peace?* I thought and nearly laughed with it. *Quiet?* My mind was a circus. But my son was sleeping soundly on me, as he had done so many nights as a child, and a short time later I felt my own breathing change in line with his. My head dropped and my eyes became heavy and

I must have fallen asleep along with him, because the next thing I can recall from that night is the morning after: the awkward crick of my neck, the slow stir of waking, and the impact of horror when I remembered everything that had passed between us the night before.

Otis woke soon after I did, as though our bodies were somehow still tuned to the same inward clock. He rubbed at his eyes too hard and when he pulled his hands away, the red pockets beneath them were swollen and, I thought, probably sore to touch as well.

'You should call in sick for work, sweet–'

'I can't take a day off,' he snapped, the old Otis having stepped back in the room. I don't know what expression I made, but it encouraged something like sympathy in him. When he spoke again his tone had changed; not quite boyhood, but certainly not businessman anymore either. 'I'm sorry, Mum, you... I shouldn't be speaking to you like that, you deserve...' he petered out and reached into his front pocket. When he pulled out his phone I could see there were missed calls, text messages and emails waiting for him; I wondered how many of them might be from work, or Emilia. 'I'll call work.'

I squeezed his knee before I stood. 'What would you like for breakfast?'

Otis groaned and rubbed at his forehead. 'I feel hungover.'

'So something with toast?'

A sharp laugh fell out of him and I wondered whether he might snap again. 'You're such a mum sometimes, do you know that?'

I leaned forward and kissed his head. 'I'm your mother, always.'

By the time Otis joined me in the kitchen I was plating up egg and soldiers for him. I no longer knew my son well enough to know whether he preferred fried, poached, scrambled;

whether he scattered protein powder over his food like a garnish, as so many young people seemed to now. But after the evening he'd had, and the desperately needed sleep that followed, a soft-boiled egg and strips of white toast with lashings of butter was the only comfort I could think of. He smiled when he saw the plate waiting on the table for him, and I thought that I had, perhaps, got something right. I finished making our tea and then joined him. I couldn't stomach food yet, but no child of mine would ever leave my home hungry. My rear had hardly touched the seat when I leapt up and fetched salt from the cupboard, and ketchup from the fridge.

'I don't have brown sauce,' I said as I set both condiments on the table.

'That's because it's disgusting.'

Some things never change, I thought with a sincere smile, and then I sat opposite my son again. He took one slim soldier and dunked it into his egg as though that action was being performed under duress; I imagined someone holding a gun to his head, forcing him to chew through the meal or else. *But at least it isn't a pillow to the face,* I thought with a thump of a swallow. Of course, I hadn't seen what Otis had done to Lucy that night. But I would always know, now, I would always carry that with me – even as I watched him warm to his favourite childhood meal, suddenly sinking soldiers into the overflowing egg cup and putting them into his mouth whole. There was a streak of sunshine-yellow yolk at the corner of his mouth. I wanted to lick my thumb and wipe him clean.

'Do you want more?' I asked, still staring at the egg on his face.

He shook his head to decline the offer. 'No, thank you, honestly.'

We both upheld a quiet while Otis finished eating. He either hadn't noticed that I hadn't cooked for myself, or he was too hungry to care. Either way, I was glad to have sidestepped the question. When all of this was over, I decided, I would take him and his brother out for McDonald's; I would recapture their innocence somehow, in a Happy Meal package. For now, I could only nurse my tea and stare into the drink as though the bubbles of milk on top might crystal-ball reveal an answer to all of this; a signpost, signalling what I was expected to do next. I was still appraising the culture of three bubbles when, in my peripheral vision, I saw Otis wipe his mouth clean on the sleeve of his jumper. If he were a boy, I would snatch the clothing off him and throw it straight into the machine to rid the wool of snot and tears and yolk. I wondered whether Emilia did the washing in their house, or whether they shared the duty. I wanted to ask then, but somehow I knew it wasn't altogether important. Besides which, there were bigger questions to entertain, like, what will Edward do with this faux confession and–

'Mum, what happens now?'

Otis yanked me out of the thought. I stretched across the table to him and rested my hand palm up. He rested his hand inside mine and I squeezed. 'I honestly don't know...'

The box of documents, printouts, pictures and testimonials relating to Lucy was sitting in the back of my car. I had driven to the police station three times in the last two days, each time with the intention of handing the materials back to Rule and telling her I couldn't be party to this fight any longer. I had done my time, I would tell her. But each time I arrived at the station car park I found that I was sweating and shaking and talking myself out of the process. I told myself that I had to go through with Edward; though I no longer knew what that meant, or what end I was hoping for. There had been a distinct shift between desperately wanting to find Lucy and desperately hoping no one ever did – because if they did, they might be able to tell, even now, that she hadn't been killed in the same way the others had. And if she hadn't been killed in the same way the others had, then Edward must be telling the truth. And if Edward were telling the truth then there must be another kil–

Knock-knock.

My head had been resting on the top of my steering wheel but I snapped upright at the sound. Kitsell was standing outside my car, wearing a tight-lipped smile and a concerned frown. He gestured for me to roll the window down but I opened the door instead.

'Maggie, is everything okay?'

I forced a laugh. 'Yes, yes, absolutely. I...' I needed to think of an excuse faster; I needed to have a bank of them ready and pocketed in my jeans for occasions such as this one. 'I've been having trouble with my phone,' I eventually managed, 'I've been trying to get hold of you all for days but the bloody thing is useless. I didn't know what else to do apart from...' The sentence died in my mouth as the station door opened ahead of us and Rule, Thompson and Newell came tumbling out.

'We're actually going to the prison.'

I forced myself to look back at him. 'You're seeing Edward?'

'Mm,' Kitsell nodded, 'you're welcome to...'

'Maggie,' Rule chimed in when she'd closed the distance to us, 'are you here for...' She laughed. 'Sorry, what are you here for?'

'Maggie's phone has broken; she came to have a chat with us the old-fashioned way instead.' Kitsell's frown loosened as he spoke to his colleague. He stepped away from my door then, too, and I soon realised he was encouraging me out of the car. 'I've told her she's welcome to visit Edward with us, if she wants to. That's okay, DI Rule, isn't it?'

Rule shrugged. 'The more the merrier.'

Even by Rule's standards she seemed chilled towards me.

'May I speak with him, when we get there?' I asked as I climbed out of the car.

'About Lucy and about Lucy only?' Rule said and I nodded in agreement. 'Then by all means, you're welcome to.'

There was something violent turning over in my stomach by then. I wedged my hands into the pockets of my coat, to hide the slight stammer that they'd developed, and I followed the detectives to their cars. Kitsell and Thompson moved towards one, while Rule and Newell opted for another. I didn't know which vehicle would be safest. I had lost comradeship with Rule, it seemed, or it felt so at least. But I felt sure, too, that Kitsell would try to draw a conversation out of me if I chose that mode of transport. Faced off against a conversation, Rule suddenly felt like the better option of the two. Wordlessly, I followed her and Newell to their car and climbed into the back.

Newell was driving while Rule was thumbing through a folder of documents. I tried to peer over without being seen, to pry at what she was looking through. If they were planning to see Edward whether I was with them or not, I could only assume there was a reason for it. Did they have more information? Or were they still blindly searching for the secret that Edward had kept stashed under his prison bunk for so long? I was balanced on this knife-edge of wanting to ask but not wanting to seem overly curious. *But isn't it* more *suspicious not to ask?* I goaded myself, and a sigh-sound tumbled out of me, loud enough to catch Rule's attention. She turned to me then, and to my surprise she smiled.

'We want to know who the killer is.'

'I'm sorry?'

The comment, unprompted and unattached to any more information, felt like a sudden slap around the face. I resisted the urge to lift my hand and check for lacerations.

'If Edward didn't kill Lucy, as he claims, then someone else did.'

I forced myself to swallow and buy a second before answering. 'Why do you think Edward knows who the killer is?'

Rule narrowed her eyes at my question before turning and slumping back in her seat. She stared out of her window as she answered. 'Because the bastard clearly knows something.' There was a long pause before she added, 'And he seems to think you do, too...'

THIRTY-ONE

They were not the ideal circumstances under which to practise the lie. There were two detectives watching me, two former detectives, and my husband. There may have been guards, even, stashed in their own corners of the prison watching on their cameras. But it was my husband – *ex*-husband, I had started to correct myself again – and his searching stare that caused the most pressure. Edward and I had been trapped in our confines for twenty minutes already and he had rebuffed my efforts to talk about Lucy every time I had approached the subject of her. 'Why do we *always* have to talk about Lucy?' He sounded like a tired husband being tormented by questions relating to a one-night stand, rather than a murderer making his final confessions. Though of course, I reminded myself again, Lucy wasn't his confession to make.

Edward leaned forward and used his fingertip to trace a pattern on the table. The grease of his skin left the ghost of something behind. 'Can we talk about when I die?'

'That's not what I'm here to talk about.' I tried to keep a stone face, a steady voice, even though the question had chilled me. 'You have a prison pastor for that.'

He flattened his hand and banged it against the metal tabletop as best as he could. It was a weak gesture and I wondered whether the cancer had started to numb his muscles. 'Maggie, don't be so fucking heartless,' he snapped, and he sounded sincerely hurt. 'I've given you all everything you wanted.'

'You haven't given us Lucy.'

He tilted his head and nearly smiled; there was a twitch in the left side of his mouth, I noticed, but it didn't become fully formed. 'You really don't know?'

'Edward, I–'

'You *really* don't know?'

I matched his gesture and leaned forwards onto the table. Our elbows were nearly touching. It was the closest we'd come to physical contact since the day he was arrested. I thought I heard his breath catch in his throat. The closeness was enough to make my skin itch, a small prickle of hives creeping beneath my cardigan, but I needed them to believe this performance. In the same way Edward had acted, I, too, needed to act now; I needed everyone to believe that I didn't know. Maybe I needed to make myself believe it, too.

'I really... don't... know.' I spoke with a deliberate and weighted pause between each word. 'Are you going to tell me?'

'Where she is,' he leaned back in his seat and clutched at his side as he moved, 'or who did it?'

'Both.'

He slowly shook his head. 'I need a painkiller.'

'You and me both.' My answer seemed to cut him, and I was spitefully glad of it. 'Are you going to tell me who murdered Lucy?'

Edward forced out a long stream of air and dropped his head back. I wondered whether he understood what I was asking him; not, are you going to tell me, but rather, are you going to tell them? I wanted to believe it would be pointless now. That if he wanted them to know, he would have told them so already. He'd barely even told me, after all; only left a trail of moulded breadcrumbs to follow instead. Now, Edward stared up at the ceiling as though searching for something there, and he didn't answer me for what felt like a long time. I was painfully aware of the blood pumping in my ears, my heartbeat creeping higher and the sound of it deepening, leaving a hollow thrum in my body. The longer his silence lasted, the more worried I became that the beating drum in me might become audible to everyone else.

'I can't tell you, Maggie.' He righted himself then and looked back at me. 'I can't.'

I nodded, slowly, and tried to suppress a look of what I thought must be relief. Of course, I hadn't expected him to say Otis's name. But I couldn't altogether rule out the possibility either; not until this, not until now. The volume dial of my heartbeat turned down one, two notches, and I nodded again.

'Can you tell anyone?'

Edward looked to think on that question, too, for a moment, before he shook his head.

'Can you tell anyone where she is?'

'I won't tell anyone where she is.'

I sighed. It was relief again, but I hoped to God it sounded like frustration. I needed to feign anger, outrage, impatience, but the closer we got to establishing that yes, my son was safe, the more inclined I felt to lean across the table and hug my husband's ailing body close to me and whisper thank you – no matter the nervous outbreak and itch it would cause in me. *If anything is going to give this away, it will be that,* I reminded myself with a curt reprimand; I needed to hold the façade.

'Then we're done, aren't we?'

Edward looked saddened by that. It was still in me,

somewhere in the well of my stomach, to comfort him when something irked him, or pained him. I supposed it was a muscle memory, or an emotional equivalent. How could anyone spend years soothing the ills of another, applying balms and soft touches to their tenderest parts, only then to disregard them in their final moments of need? And these were, of course, Edward's final moments. If he hadn't been in prison – *if he hadn't been a murderer,* I amended – we would be sitting in our home making to-do lists for his death. It seemed a redundant suggestion now, to propose that we note down everything that needed to happen, or everything that needed to be done. Edward was a care of state. He would be hospitalised if he required it. He would see a priest or pastor if he asked for one. And he would slip away quietly without any of us knowing, until a phone call came with the news – or a headline.

I swallowed a shaky breath at the thought. 'I think it's time I go.'

'Maggie, come on, we still have things to talk about.' He sounded pleading in a way that I didn't recognise in him. It made it harder to hate him, harder to leave. 'How are the boys? Are they doing okay?'

I wondered whether it was a pointed question. Was he asking me whether I'd confronted our son? Slapped the backs of his knees and docked his money for a week? It was impossible to know. There was a circus of suspicion and anxiety and scepticism banging cymbals in a disorganised circle around the outskirts of my brain. That had become my baseline way of thinking, feeling, now. But for his faults – *oh, Maggie, what an understatement* – he looked sincere, then; he looked as though he were truly pleading for an answer.

I managed a sad smile. 'The boys are fine, Edward. But they aren't–'

'Would they see me, do you think?' His eyes narrowed as he

fixed the question on me, and somehow it felt as though he were asking something else entirely. 'To wish me luck and wave me goodbye?' The shift in tone from desperate to jovial was awkward and false. But at least it was easier to deny him the ask when he sounded like this.

Otis and I had talked at length about whether he would see his father, whether it was even safe for him to. One bad meeting, and we both feared that Edward's loyalty might collapse into a more proper confession, something that there was no coming back from. It wasn't worth the risk – and if Edward was anything, he was certainly a risk factor. Meanwhile, Finn had only given me confusion in response to the same query – 'Why would I want to see him?' – which I took to be an answer in itself. I'd asked Finn out of politeness, of course, habit: never give to one son without the other, even when the thing being given was an opportunity to meet their murderer of a father one last time. But something in me had been ready for Edward to ask, when he sensed we were nearing the end of our time together, and I couldn't be sure that in the light of everything, now, whether Otis might have changed his mind. Did he feel a new fondness for Edward? Was this something they shared, now, openly? I'd wondered. It wasn't quite fishing or trainspotting or a deep-rooted love of a movie franchise; it wasn't any of the things that I'd idly wished my son might share with his father, when we'd found out we were having our first boy. But still, it was something in them both. My stomach rolled over at the thought of what our poor boy might have inherited.

I shook my head and made eye contact with the table rather than him. The swell of feelings in me was both too big and too overlapping – sympathy, pity, hate, gratitude – for me to look at him now. I worried which of the feelings would come tumbling out.

'I suppose that's fair,' he answered, 'after everything I've put them through.'

'You were a good father, Edward.' The sentence erupted, fully formed and soft. I still couldn't look at him. 'You're a terrible person,' I added, as though to counter the sentimentality of the comment that came before it, 'but you were always a good dad.'

Owing to my fixed stare on the table, I didn't realise Edward had moved closer to me. In fact, it didn't occur to me at all until I felt the cold, dry skin of his hand clasped around my own. And in a single swift movement that reminded us both of our roles in this, I snatched my hand back, dropped both into my lap and stared at him, instead of the metal that separated us, and I slowly shook my head. A quiet dismissal, clear but not unkind, I hoped, and Edward looked as though he understood.

'You really won't tell anyone what happened to Lucy, where she is even?' I couldn't help but ask the question again, if only so Rule could see that I'd tried. I didn't know whether it was lip service for the benefit of those I knew were watching, or whether I really needed the additional reassurance one last time – perhaps it was a medley of both. It had always frustrated Edward that I could never seek a guarantee just the one time; it was always something I went back for. Every expensive household item we bought, I checked the paperwork at least three times before agreeing to the purchase. This question wasn't entirely dissimilar to taking home a new oven system or a boiler; both had the potential to blow up my home.

Edward shook his head. 'I've told you lot enough,' he cast an eye towards the mirror-window then, 'you know everything you're going to know.'

'Then we really are done.' I pushed back from the table and resisted the urge to shake Edward's hand, as though this were a civil series of meetings that had taken place. 'Take care of yourself, Edward, won't you?'

He laughed. 'Yep, the cancer and I will take care.'

Of course, my sentiment had been foolish, but what proper goodbye would there have been? I quietly trod to the door then and waited for the click of it unlocking. In those laboured seconds, where I tried desperately not to turn and look, not to give my husband the satisfaction of another glance, Edward spoke again.

'If they call you, at the end, will you come?'

The door opened and there was Rule. She flashed me a smile, a warmer one than she had done earlier in the day, and I took that as validation for something. I turned back into the space but still didn't look at Edward.

'No, I won't.'

I decided I'd punished myself quite enough, now. There was such a thing as too much penance.

***

Rule made me a strong cup of tea and seated me in the quiet of her office. From across the desk she blew on her own drink, and a smog of coffee rolled over the lip of the mug and towards me. I should have asked for a latte, I realised then, and I wondered whether I could justify the indulgence of stopping for one somewhere on the way home. Rule took two measured sips of her drink before deciding, I guessed, that it was too hot still, before she put it down on a pile of cardboard folders that were sitting on the corner of her desk. *They can't all be about Edward,* I thought – or perhaps hoped – as I cradled my tea and took further glances around the room. She was a busy woman, that much was evident from the space she kept, and I wondered whether she could warrant any more time trying to crack the case of my husband, or whether this might signal an end for her, too.

'Are you okay?' she eventually asked, pulling my attention around to her. 'I know you and he have had some big discussions but– There seemed to be a lot of feeling involved in everything today? A lot of finality.'

I tried for a smile but I didn't put too much enthusiasm into it. 'If he isn't going to tell me where Lucy is, and he has nothing more to confess to about any others then...' I petered out and shrugged. 'He and I have nothing more to say to each other.'

Rule nodded and pulled her coffee back towards her. She only fidgeted with the cup, though, treated it as somewhere to fix her stare. 'He'd really got it into his head that you were going to work out *something* about Lucy, hadn't he?'

'Mm,' I murmured in agreement. 'But once upon a time he'd got it into his head that it was socially acceptable to murder a string of young women.' I paused to sip my tea, and Rule looked back at me in those seconds. 'It's been a long time since I understood the subtleties of my husband's thinking.'

The sentiment seemed to have caught her off guard, because she actually laughed in answer to it; a curt, abrupt noise that I think surprised us both. 'Funny, I've got an ex-husband who makes me feel much the same. Albeit for very different reasons,' she rushed to add. 'Please keep the box folder we gave you, just in case? I know it's a long shot, but...'

I nodded. 'Of course. If anything ever comes to mind.'

'Thank you, Maggie. And thank you for everything else, to date.'

I waved it off as though my efforts had been nothing – as though I hadn't lost hours of sleep, forgotten to eat, missed work deadlines, misplaced family memories and lost a son in the process of finding their dead girls. *Yes,* I thought as I took one, two sips from my tea, *yes, I've punished myself enough, now.*

THIRTY-TWO

The diaries were all in a separate box; everything from the time of Edward. I had no idea why I'd kept them for so long, but I resolved that I wouldn't keep them any longer. A month passed before I started the first fire. I waited for phone calls from Rule, Kitsell, Newell or Thompson, but they never arrived. The closest I came to a follow-up conversation with any of them was when Kitsell called me one evening, outside of typical working hours, simply to ask whether I was keeping well, taking care of myself and so on. He hadn't seen Edward again, he told me, and to the best of his knowledge neither had Rule. I knew, then, that it must be over – or as close to over as it was ever going to get. The media was still managing to make snacks and non-nutritious meals of the story, but from everything I saw my own presence was still a spectre in their storytelling. I was Edward O'Connor's wife as far as they knew. Maggie Moloney continued to live a quiet existence of work and cooking and food banks. And now, bonfires in her back garden in the crisp of winter.

I replaced the visits to Edward with working through my to-do list around the home. The house would be going on the market in the new year, and Rebecca had made no secret of the fact that no one in their right mind would buy a house that required *such* renovation work on the garden. So in the still afternoons, when I had run out of attention to work and the frost had thawed through, I took to uprooting parts of the garden. I cut back hedges, I broke branches, and I pulled flowers' feet up from the earth to make way for new planting when the weather broke. Trip by trip I had taken things to the local skip before realising a more efficient disposal would be to burn it all. It was sometime during this – the second fire in the space of a week – that I realised this would be the best way of exorcising the last of Edward from my belongings, too.

Moving the boxes from the loft to the downstairs didn't even make it onto a to-do list. As soon as the thought occurred to me, I set to lifting and shifting everything from that time in our life together. I kept the photo albums, of course, though I removed Edward's face from each binder before throwing those onto the fire in the garden. I took a picture of the roar of it and sent it to the boys in our group chat – we had a group chat by then – with a message attached that read: *Would anyone like marshmallows?*

I hoped they'd take it in good humour.

I added bramble sticks to the fire which stoked it further, then threw another binder of photographs on top. I don't know how long I waited, how long I watched it all burn through, but there was something cathartic about seeing the pages curl and wrinkle and disappear entirely. It felt better still when I started to throw the diaries into the heat. They held a mixture of memories. Some were simply days and dates when things happened. Others were lengthier documents, pages upon pages that held the remnants of a life that now, after it all, felt very much like it belonged to someone else. For some time, while I was watching the first of them itch and tumble through the bonfire, I managed to convince myself it was only fiction that I was burning through; only something that a man with a creative tongue had made up for me, and whispered year after year like a bedtime story.

It had been an hour since I'd texted the boys and neither of them had replied. It wasn't until I was in the kitchen checking my phone for them that I heard the front doorbell, though, ringing over and again with an impatience. Whoever it was, I must have kept them waiting, and I was ready with an apology rising in my throat. I anticipated a harried neighbour ready to exchange choice words about the late-in-the-day fires but instead–

'Come on, McDonald's *never* stays warm.' Finn elbowed his way into the house with two bags of food balanced between his arms. But he soon hurried back to give me a kiss on the cheek. 'Otis has the marshmallows,' he said before rushing off towards the kitchen again.

Otis waved with a bag of American marshmallows; a single one looked large enough to fill a mouth. 'I've got the drinks, too,' he said with a laugh, 'we thought we'd surprise you with the least healthy dinner you'll likely have all week.'

I tried to remember the last dinner I'd had. It may have been a cheese sandwich; it may have been yesterday or the day before. If the boys were to look, they would find the bin made up of Polo packets and half-eaten bags of Skips. Neither of them looked of course, they were too busy trying to remember who had ordered the Big Mac and who had ordered the other burger that was markedly similar to a Big Mac but more expensive.

'And it comes with extra cheese,' Finn was arguing as I followed them both in. 'Mum, do you actually want to eat in front of the open fire out there?'

'Mum,' Otis peered through the open kitchen doors, 'are you actually *allowed* to have an open fire out there?'

I shrugged. 'I'll bake Christmas cookies for the cul-de-sac.'

Since Edward, I was learning to seek a different kind of penance for my ills.

'Okay, shall we eat outside then? It would be cool to have the fire?' Finn suggested and Otis and I quietly agreed.

Finn was busy seeking trays for the food while I was puncturing the mouths of the drinks' containers, feeding the straws through and making a guess at who had chocolate milkshake and who had strawberry. I turned with one in each hand and saw Otis leaning in the doorway, staring into the garden.

'What are you burning?' he asked in a low voice when Finn was out of earshot.

I tiptoed to kiss my son's cheek. 'Everything, sweetheart. Absolutely everything...'

Finn managed to eat so many marshmallows that he was relegated to the living room for a lie down. He was sprawled on the sofa letting out the occasional whimper, loud enough to be heard in both the kitchen – where Otis was cleaning away the remains of dinner – and outside, where I was loading the last of my life into the bonfire. I hoped this might be the final blaze and I wanted to make the most of it, lest the neighbours lose their tempers or become suspicious. People watched so much true crime now, you could never be sure what they were thinking of you. Though in my case, there was a very real possibility they would be right.

I knew which one the damning diary was without looking for it. I weighed it carefully from one hand to the other, as though it were any heavier than the others I'd disposed of already. There were so many curls of black drifting up from the garden, I was beginning to worry at what state the grass beneath it would be. *But you can't fix everything at once,* I reminded myself.

'Everything okay out here?' Otis stepped out into the cold and tucked an arm around my shoulders. 'Christ, Mum, you've got a shiver on and everything.' He pulled me closer to him and for a second or two neither of us spoke; we just stared ahead, treating the fire as though it were a crystal ball that might crack open and reveal something to us.

'How's your brother?'

Otis huffed a laugh. 'He'll live.'

Now I knew – or rather, now I *knew* that I knew, because I had decided part of me must have always known, or nearly known, even – Otis and I had a better relationship than I could remember us ever having had before. I wondered whether this secret had always been a partition between us, an unhealthy distance that had collapsed in the face of its reveal. In place of that, there was a quiet bond instead; neither of us spoke of what the other knew unless it was in veiled and hushed terms, and even then we never spoke of it for long. There was, I told my son more than once, nothing left to say; the line that every forgiving parent uses when they are encouraging a child to move on from an indiscretion. Edward had disagreed, it seemed, given that he wrote to both of the boys after he and I had had our final visit. The letters came to me, through the police station, two weeks after Edward and I had said goodbye. Neither of the boys opened them though – and it wasn't my place to. They were somewhere in this fire now, care of a diary that had swallowed them and a flame that had swallowed that. *That's how easy it is to get rid of it all,* I thought, and I leaned in closer to my son.

'Emilia wanted to know if you were free for dinner on Sunday.'

'This Sunday?'

'Mm, is that okay?'

I looked down in the diary balanced between my hands. My fingertips had turned a pattern of white and purple. Otis was right; I must have been colder than I knew. I had read and reread this diary, trying every time to be sure and surer still of what I thought I knew. The date that I'd been away, that weekend, was red crayon scribbled onto my memory now like a relative's birthday or an important appointment. But it seemed that Otis had managed to forget – and somehow, I felt glad.

'What time do you want me and what can I bring?'

'And why am I not invited?' Finn's add-on came from the doorway behind us.

'He lives!' Otis threw his hands in the air in a theatrical gesture.

'Don't take the piss, I–'

'Finn, don't swear, it's unbecoming,' I cautioned him, though I winked with it. My sons were grown men now, and if this experience had taught me anything it was that I had long ago slipped past a point of being able to tell them what they could and could not, should and should not do. Still, a curt 'Ha' erupted from Otis, in a spiteful but playful tone, as he moved from me to his brother and immediately started to ruffle at his hair.

'Joke's on you,' Finn said in a surprisingly calm reaction, 'I actually prefer it like this.'

'Jesus,' Otis said under his breath but loud enough for us both to hear. 'Mum, can I drag you in for a cup of tea before hypothermia sets in?'

'Please,' I said, though I moved closer to the fire. 'Put the kettle on and I'll be in in a moment. Finn, there are biscuits in the cupboard if...' I petered out when I heard his groan. When both boys had disappeared from the doorway I turned back to the open blaze.

It was a long and winding diary. It wasn't the type with dates and meetings and places to be. Rather, it was the type that you held late at night with a cup of tea and half an hour of quiet, where you reflected on the day, documented things your children had done that had embarrassed you, the dinner you'd made and how well it went, the work your husband had been doing in the garden and the posh restaurant he took you to that one time. The entries were meticulous, detailed. And they would be all anyone needed, if anyone ever thought to look.

I threw the diary onto the fire and waited until its edges started to lift.

'Mum, come on!' Otis shouted out to me. 'We're revisiting an old classic.'

I walked back into the house in time to catch one son throwing a biscuit into my other son's mouth – and missing. The custard cream bounced off Finn's cheek and landed on the floor, landing with a small crack. I cocked an eyebrow but laughed along with them as I turned to lock the doors, and I left the fire happily smouldering on the outside.

THIRTY-THREE

Weeks rolled by again with nothing. After months of life being too much – years of it being *too* hard – it became decidedly boring instead. The house was a mess of boxes but I found I was enjoying the process of packaging up my life again; the reasoning for it felt markedly different this time to how it had during previous moves. This property hadn't sold yet but I was already in the process of buying another; a fresh home on the coast, in fact, that was an hour away from the boys, though they promised to visit regularly.

'Do you think they will?'

Rebecca was standing in my kitchen drinking wine from a plastic cup. The glassware was already in a box, somewhere, but she had assured me that it was hardly the first time and most certainly not the last that she'd drunk wine from a cup that looked as though it had come from a Happy Meal box.

I shrugged. 'I've got no idea.'

The three of us were closer now, as though the experience of my dealing with Edward had somehow worked out kinks in our relationships that we hadn't known were there – or perhaps we had known, really, we had only ignored them. Regardless, we were closer; Otis and I especially. There were times when it felt like his proximity was a way of apologising, this spending time together somehow a currency he was using to repay me for keeping his secret. But there were times, too, when it only felt like a mother and a son enjoying each other's company, and that authenticity of feeling made it easier to believe that yes, they probably would both visit. Besides which, Emilia and Alice were overjoyed by the prospect of sitting in a living room with a seafront view; so whether my sons came or not, I thought I could expect to see more of their partners.

I pushed my plate away and let out a heartfelt sigh. Food had become a soft joy again, and Rebecca's suggestion of curry with all the trimmings had been a welcome one after another day of shifting between packing and writing. Despite promising myself that I would give up smoking, again, when food became easier, I found that I was crossing to the kitchen drawer where my half-empty box lived out of sight; a dessert to a warming meal.

Rebecca narrowed her eyes at me as I placed a cigarette between my lips.

'Don't give me that look.' I held the packet out towards her.

'If you can't beat them,' she said as she took one and came to stand by the doorway with me. I parted the doors just enough to let the smoke out, but not so far open that the December cold came rushing in. 'I wasn't actually judging you for the smoking though,' she added as I held a lighter out towards her. She leaned forward and touched the end of her cigarette to it.

'No?' I lit my own. 'What were you judging me for?'

She laughed. 'I was thinking, there's something different about you.'

She was right, of course, there was. I couldn't tell her what; I'm not sure I knew entirely myself. But like a shedding of something, a skin left behind, it felt very much like I was moving towards a life that was untouched by Edward, and that seemed to make all the difference. I no longer slowed down for amber lights; I had lied to work about a doctor's appointment to avoid attending an online meeting; I had cancelled a meeting with Sarah under the pretence of having a horrid cold when in truth, I simply hadn't wanted to go. Admittedly, I was still attending the food bank – with more meals than ever, given that I was clearing through three years' worth of tins in my kitchen cupboards – and I was donating much of my life to charity, having vowed to share out the wealth of things I no longer needed. One of those things that I was only too happy to discard, I had recently decided, was guilt. And it was nothing short of miraculous what the sloughing of that did to a person.

I exhaled into the garden, not knowing what was smoke and what was winter chill. 'I'm upping and moving to the seaside,' I shrugged, 'perhaps that changes a person.'

'Well,' Rebecca inhaled hard and I heard the crackle of it, 'while I'm not altogether happy that you're moving even further away, it's good to see the change in you, Mags. You seem...' She narrowed her eyes and looked hard for the right word choice. 'Lighter.'

'Funny.' I leaned outside to dab the cigarette out on the wall. 'That's how I feel.'

Of course, it was easy to feel light, airy, lifted even during the daylight hours, and even the early evening ones, when there was company to busy myself with and to-do lists to tick off entries for, work assignments still to complete. The harder hours were the ones that followed. It was two days after Rebecca's visit in a late, late and lonely hour – the real witching hour, I had decided – when things simply became too much again. Like a tide thrashing against a seawall's curve in the midst of winter, not guilt but something like it launched itself at the shaped walls of my stomach. I scrunched my eyes closed and concentrated on my breathing as though I could relax the ill feelings away. Though I knew from bitter experience and years of arduous practice that it was unlikely to be so easy. I imagined a square, a triangle; I tried to stretch each breath down to my stomach where the high tide was still lapping at the shores of my thinking. And after what felt like hours of this – though in truth it had been only thirty-two minutes – I heaved myself out of bed, swallowed the sea spit and bile that rose with the gesture, and I felt through the darkness until I found my clothes. There was one thing left to do that might cause the storm to abate, and for no clear reason at all this felt like the time to try it.

Every movement was completed with care to detail. I closed my front door softly so as not to disturb the neighbours; I crept to the car like a villain from a cartoon; then I held my breath while I slammed the car door closed, willing the empty windows around me to stay that way, praying there weren't people awake enough to twitch at their curtains and question me. It took nearly an hour, driving in the general direction of my old home – our first and only home, as a family – until I found an all-night garage that still had a sparse display of flowers on its forecourt. Admittedly, flowers were an unlikely purchase for anyone in the early hours of the morning, I knew that, but I had still hoped for something more promising than bright yellows and limp reds. I ended up buying three bouquets – though the term feels generous – and compiling them into a single bunch, leaving scraps of green and shards of thorn on my passenger seat to remove later. It felt like evidence of something.

It took another two hours to get home; not *my* home, but the old home, a cul-de-sac landscape we had been forced to vacate when I was denying knowledge of my husband's crimes, and trying to shield my boys from the media frenzy of it all. There had been a quick injunction the first time around that prevented their names from being published – Edward O'Connor, father of two, was as much as any reader knew for certain – and this second time, they had both simply been lucky. But driving back here for the first time in years felt like exposing the wound of it – inviting the badness back in.

I parked my car on the fringes of the street and idled for a minute. The houses all looked different somehow even though structurally they were much the same. The home we had lived in was lived in by someone else now. There were two cars on the driveway, and a third floor – an attic conversion, I guessed – that had been done in the twenty years since us. *It must be a family there now,* I thought, and that somehow warmed and chilled me at once. In the centre of these houses, though, with their closed curtains and their dim lights, there remained the community garden project. Twenty years old, too, but it still bloomed with colour even in this winterscape, and the flowers there, while frosted, held their own kind of beauty. It had been such a challenge for the neighbours to work together, when an old tree was culled from the centre of the street, but after *many* meetings – some of which had been held in my front room, as it was then – we had decided to make the empty surface green. Plant flowers, a small hedge, root a cement statue for decoration; though the intricacies of these things had inevitably led to more arguments.

Edward's interest had quickly moved from nearly non-existent through to embarrassingly enthusiastic. He became the chief wrangler in the end, digging and pruning long after others had given up for the day. At the time, I mistook his interest in the project for community spirit. Now, I understood it as fatherly instinct. From the cloudy windscreen of my car I stared out at the centre portion of land, owned by no one in particular, but clearly still cared for by many – and I wondered where Lucy was, exactly.

It had been so late one evening when I'd found Edward working out there. I'd crept from bed, expecting to find him downstairs watching television or frowning over a crossword. But when I had exhausted my inspection of all the rooms, and come away with empty hands, I had finally thought to look outside. And there he was, with sweat on his brow and a small, free-standing light wedged into the freshly overturned ground.

'What on earth are you doing?' I'd asked, my voice a hurried whisper at the time.

Twenty years later, I knew. Though he must have buried her before that, I thought. Which meant that when I found him, he was only visiting...

That familiar feeling of guilt settled over me when I climbed out of the car. I took the flowers with me but, wary of drawing suspicion, I only laid them at the side of the road, near the entryway to the cul-de-sac. I worried at the questions that might be asked, if they were left on the centre landscape itself. Here, they looked as though they were honouring the victim of a car crash; someone who had taken the corner too quickly and perished as a result. I didn't mind that. But still, having laid them there, I wandered along the pavement until I came to the point of crossing to get to the centre garden. I thought of sitting, taking a moment to draw in the scenery, christen the bench that I'd never used. The thought of walking over Lucy's grave stopped me.

Instead, I lingered on the edge and crouched. My fingers worried at the fringes of earth, upturned from recent work, perhaps. Someone would find her, one day, I knew that much. But whether there would be enough left of her to tie her to my son, rather than my husband, I felt less sure of. Otis had told me how he had grabbed at the pillow, how he had pressed. With the ghost of that conversation sitting alongside me I reached for my own throat then, and struggled down a swallow as though a similar pressure had been applied to me. Strangulation had been Edward's method. I hated the connective tissue between their techniques.

'I am so deeply, deeply sorry,' I said to no one and nothing in particular. 'I am deeply sorry for everything they did to you.' I was not religious, and hadn't been since girlhood. But still, I made the mark of the cross, tapping my fingertips top and bottom, left and right. 'God keep you safe,' I struggled to stand then, 'and may God forgive us this.'

My grandmother had once told me that whether a person is religious or not, they will always ask for a god when they need one. I needed one, then. I needed one on the unsteady walk back to the car, and I needed one as I shrugged off my shroud of guilt and left it there, next to the flowers I had brought. This was the last of it, I decided. This was where Lucy lay, or had been lain – and this would be the last time I would think of the girl my son had murdered.

THIRTY-FOUR

In honour of my final shift at the food bank, I had decided to sacrifice my usual nutrition-conscious meals and I had instead baked four cakes: a Victoria sponge, a lemon drizzle, a carrot and walnut, and a blueberry and banana. Claire's face had lit up in equal parts surprise and delight when I had walked in with one cake box balanced on another, and she had belched out a curt laugh when I explained there were another two still to come. Meanwhile, my own emotions were balanced between delight and relief when three of the earliest visitors to my makeshift cake stand happened to be the same single mother, with both of her children trailing behind her. Their enthusiasm spiked when they saw that they were walking into a veritable feast of sugar, though, and I was only too happy to oblige them with a small piece from each cake.

'If that's okay?' I asked their mum, though my knife had already scored through a walnut.

She nodded. 'Of course.'

I cut small triangles and set them on paper plates for the boys. 'Would you like...'

She held up a hand. 'I'm okay, thank you.'

'Not even a...' I pointed to the blueberry option. 'It really is quite nice.'

'Oh, just a small piece,' she laughed along, 'to be sociable.'

'A small piece, that I can do.' Though it was clear that I couldn't, when I handed her over a slice of cake that could only be described as a wedge.

'Are you celebrating something?'

I was still getting used to sharing the information. The boys knew, as did Rebecca; work had no need to know, owing to every assignment being remote working; Kitsell and Thompson I had told, too, of course, though I had done so through a change-of-address card sent care of the police station. Somehow, it hadn't felt right to call either of them with the news. With perfect strangers, though, I was still acclimatising to the comfort of being able to share my life without the worry of an unwanted thread leading back to me for something. I had spent so many years being someone, keeping something hidden; now, though, there seemed very little left to hide. Even Edward, as evidenced by the slow ebbing of newspaper headlines, had ceased to be interesting again.

'I'm actually moving away. This will be my last shift volunteering.'

'Oh no,' she answered, with a small clump of sugar clinging to the crease of her lip, 'I mean, of course, that's lovely. But how often do you meet people who are kind to you just because they're a kind...' she petered out and shook her head. 'That sounds ridiculous, I'm sure. But since that first time we met you, I've thought– You were just a bit of a guardian angel that day, that's all.'

Feelings pricked at the corners of my eyes; gentle and warm. 'That's a very kind thing to say... I'm sorry, I never actually got your name?'

She wiped her candied hand on her coat and left a faint white stain there. 'Louise.'

'Maggie,' I answered. I returned her handshake and tried harder than I had had to in weeks not to think of the girl. 'I have two boys of my own,' I nodded to hers in the background, their mouths covered in joy and icing sugar, 'older than yours, but still just as excited by cake.'

She laughed. 'They never grow out of it then?'

'Would you want them to?'

Louise weighed up the question. 'No, probably not.' She tucked another piece of cake into her mouth and spoke around it. 'Are you moving alone, with a husband or...'

'No, only me.'

And if I sound delighted, it's because–

'The boys' dad, he isn't around?' she asked then, and I felt a little like Louise had overstepped, a little like Louise had kicked a casket of feeling buried deep in me somewhere, a little like I wanted to take my cake back.

But of course, she didn't know.

'He hasn't been for some time now, no. Only me.'

'Nothing wrong with that, is there?' She sounded defiant. 'I sometimes think that if their dad weren't sitting on the sidelines, it'd be that bit easier to get along with things. He's a– Well, I shouldn't say it really, and I'd never say it in front of them but he's a bit of a deadbeat.'

I smiled like I understood; to a degree, I did.

'It's a shame we can't lock them up and throw away the key sometimes, isn't it?' I made sure that I sounded jovial with the suggestion. But of course, I meant it. 'Can I get you anything else, from any of the other–'

'Maggie,' Claire spoke over me and interrupted my offer, 'can I steal you for a second?'

Louise turned to check for the boys. 'I'd better get them

some actual food.' She reached across for my hand and, far from the human contact causing a flinch and twitch how it might once have done, I felt immediately warmed by the gesture again. 'Thank you. Enjoy that new life of yours, wherever you're going.'

I smiled and squeezed her hand, and I hoped she wouldn't notice the stray tear that escaped from the corner of one eye. 'You take very good care of yourself, Louise.'

'I can do that.' She turned to Claire then. 'Sorry for keeping her.'

Claire tucked an arm around my shoulders when Louise had moved along, and she pulled me to her in a tight hug. 'You're going to be so missed, Maggie.'

I looked around the room; full to the brim already, only an hour into the shift, with people I both recognised and didn't. But largely, full of people who I would likely never see again. Nothing made a person realise how fleeting their life really was like rubbing elbows with strangers. It didn't matter whether I was here, and holding hands with that thought there came another: *It no longer matters what I've done.*

'Anyway, come with me, lady, if you please.' Claire stepped out from behind my station and headed in the direction of the volunteers' room. She checked to see that I was behind her before throwing the door open and, joined by a chorus of other voices, shouted, 'Surprise!'

The room was decorated with banners, balloons and small gift bags. People were hurrying in and out, moving to and from their stations, but making the most of this brief moment to say hello and goodbye in a swift motion. There were people in that room who, somehow, I didn't even know the names of; though we'd tested each other's cooking and asked, albeit in passing, about each other's days. I stared around the redecorated space – 'Bon voyage!' brandished across a sparkly banner here, and another one there – and felt such a swell of feeling that it was inevitable, unavoidable, that it would come tumbling–

'Oh, Maggie.' Claire pulled me to her again. 'This is too much?'

I wiped my eyes on the edge of my jumper. 'It's just right, it really is. It's just...'

'More than you expected?' Claire handed me a tissue with a sympathetic smile.

'It's more than I deserve.'

'Hm, no.'

My head snapped round, and I laughed at Claire's blank expression. 'Just... no?'

'Just no.'

'Well, I think–'

'Well, I *know* it definitely isn't more than you deserve. So come on,' she looped arms with me, 'I know you brought cake but so did we and we need to get a move on before the vultures finish landing.'

And just like that, the ill feelings were rebuffed and instead there was only warmth. There were gentle questions – 'Yes, right by the coast.' – and people who seemed sincerely interested in the answers – 'I'm not sure I've ever even seen that part of the country, you know?' – and there were mouths full of kindness, swapping sentiment and soft things – 'Claire is right, you really will be missed.' I managed to cry only three more times in the forty minutes that I was inside the room, with a flurry of volunteers coming and going, and Claire assured me that yes, my face was still fit for front of house in the main serving hall after the tears, too.

I spent my final shift serving slabs of cake to people who likely hadn't had a treat in months. And I couldn't think of a more worthwhile endeavour. When the cake stand had run dry, Claire unleashed me back into the world, clutching a bundle of gift bags and cards. She offered to move the balloons into the car, too, but I politely declined the offer.

'You don't know what you're missing,' she said, leaning against my open door, 'those things are full of helium.'

I remembered my boys and their desperate plea for helium balloons at every birthday party we hosted for them. At the end of the evening, Edward would always be the first to crack a seam, inhale and speak in a high-pitched tone that didn't belong to him. It was only ever the four of us by that time in the night, too, and even now they remained my favourite moments in every party we hosted. *There are some memories worth keeping,* I reminded myself.

'You know the woman I was talking to, with the boys?' Claire nodded in answer. 'Give them to her. They've had about enough sugar to make the most of some helium, I'd guess.'

'You're a good sort, Maggie.'

I smiled. 'I'm trying to be.'

'My number is in the farewell card,' Claire added then. 'Don't be a stranger?'

'Never. Bad pennies always come home.' I winked at her and she moved away from my door, giving me space to slam it closed. And I drove home with the satisfaction that this could be another thing ticked off the final to-do list that was pinned to my fridge door.

I drove home on autopilot, but now, it happened for the right reasons. There were gift bags rattling around in the back seat the entire way, and my thoughts were preoccupied with quiet wondering at what people would have bought me; what clutter I might be taking to my new seafront home, where the air was slick with salt and the beach was clean of– *Memories.* There had never been a family holiday there, which made it the perfect destination for one final new life.

I indicated and turned into my street, with a rustle of

excitement at the thought of brewing tea – that I would have to drink in a travel mug – and parting the lips of presents. But first– *There are visitors*, I realised as I pulled to a stop on my driveway. Kitsell and Thompson had parked on the road; I'd recognised their car from a clear distance. Both of the detectives were lingering on my doorstep as though not convinced that I wasn't home. I realised Kitsell was staring at his phone then, and I wondered whether there would be a missed call on mine when I finally got around to checking it. It had been in my handbag on silent since the beginning of my volunteer shift. Now though, I left that bag, and the accompanying gift bags, lying in the car while I climbed out. I caught Thompson's attention when I slammed the door closed, and Kitsell soon looked around with a smile, too. The three of us swapped something like nervous laughter, hesitant joy, unsure of how to greet each other in these moments. Inwardly, one small thought chased its tail around my head; the same squirrel trying to catch the same elusive acorn:

It's happened then. He's finally died.

Edward O'Connor 2 August 1965 – 27 January 2024. Edward passed away peacefully after a battle with cancer. He is survived by two sons. Funeral services will be private and for immediate family only. Those wishing to honour Edward's life are encouraged to make donations to the End Cancer Project in his honour.

<u>Suspense Thrillers:</u>

Intention

All I See Is You

Sincerely, Yours

The Things I Didn't Do

Safe Word

Penance

The Good Child

A True Crime

Crime:

The DI Melanie Watton Series

The Copycat (book one)

The Watcher (book two)

The Cutter (book three)